When she started searching the third compartment of the bag, Nash asked, "Need any help?"

"I appreciate that, but I know what I'm looking for."

Naturally, she found the pins in the last place she looked—at the bottom of a small zippered pocket on the inside of the diaper bag. As she pulled out the pins, her fingertips encountered something unfamiliar.

"What in the world?" She extracted a small black square about the size of a key fob. "I didn't put this in here. Kind of looks like a personal alarm my grandma carries. Except I don't have one."

"Can I see it?"

She passed him the object, concern growing. "Do you know what it is? Must have been in there a while."

He turned the object over in his hand. "Who's had access to your diaper bag?"

"No one."

"What about the marshal?"

Kiera shook her head. "The bag's been with me the entire time." Her pulse started to beat triple time. "Why? What is it?"

"I could be wrong. I'm no expert. But I think it's a tracking device."

Cathy McDavid is truly blessed to have been penning Westerns and small town stories for Harlequin since 2005. With over fifty titles in print and 1.5 million books sold, Cathy is also a member of the prestigious Romance Writers of America's Honor Roll. This "almost" Arizona native and mother of grown twins is married to her own real-life sweetheart. After leaving the corporate world seven years ago, she now spends her days penning stories about good-looking cowboys riding the range, busting broncs and sweeping gals off their feet—oops, no. Make that winning the hearts of feisty, independent women who give the cowboys a run for their money. It's a tough job, but she's willing to make the sacrifice.

Blizzard Refuge

CATHY McDAVID

LOVE INSPIRED

INSPIRATIONAL ROMANCE

LOVE INSPIRED®
INSPIRATIONAL ROMANCE

Recycling programs
for this product may
not exist in your area.

ISBN-13: 978-1-335-42617-8

Blizzard Refuge

Copyright © 2022 by Cathy McDavid Books, LLC

For questions and comments about the quality of this book, please contact us at CustomerService@Harlequin.com.

Love Inspired
22 Adelaide St. West, 41st Floor
Toronto, Ontario M5H 4E3, Canada
www.LoveInspired.com

Printed in U.S.A.

The Lord is my strength and my shield;
my heart trusted in him, and I am helped;
therefore my heart greatly rejoiceth;
and with my song will I praise Him.
—*Psalm* 28:7

To my mother. Thank you for your unwavering love even when I tested your patience, the lessons you taught me, the laughs we shared, the songs we sang together, the exciting adventures we had, the wonderful memories and for showing me the meaning of true courage through example. I miss you. I will always miss you. You are my sunshine.

Chapter One

A gust of wind slammed into the unmarked gray sedan and sent it sliding across the icy road into the opposite lane. In the back seat, Kiera Driscoll reached for her seven-month-old daughter in the car seat beside her. As if that would make any difference in a head-on collision. She was helpless to protect either of them.

"Please, God, watch over us," she whispered, every muscle in her body tensing. "Keep us safe from harm."

At the wheel, US Marshal Delana Gifford forced the car back into the correct lane. Her plain features, normally unreadable, knotted with determination as the car fishtailed, first left and then right.

Kiera sucked in a breath, squeezed her eyes shut and waited for the crash. It didn't come, and a moment later they drifted to a standstill at the side of the road.

"Thank you," she murmured.

Outside, sleet pelted the car from all angles. The windshield wipers thumped as they labored to keep up with the assault.

Marshal Gifford cranked her head around to peer

at Kiera and her daughter in the back seat. "Are you two okay?"

"I think so."

Kiera glanced down at little Heather, who somehow appeared oblivious to their nerve-racking ordeal. She gurgled contentedly and waved a bright yellow rattle in the air.

"Yes. We're fine." Kiera stroked her daughter's satiny cheek with trembling fingers.

Why had she agreed to come on this trip? What if, after countless hours of contemplation, prayer and soul-searching, she'd made the wrong decision?

No. Testifying against her husband's killer was the right thing to do. The man should be made to pay for his crime. More important, he must never be allowed to kill again. Given his high-ranking position in the 7-Crowns Syndicate, the southwest's most powerful crime organization, it was a strong possibility.

"Let's keep moving," Marshal Gifford said and eased the car forward.

Kiera peered out the windshield but could barely see anything through the storm. Until today, her greatest fear had been the target on her back, put there by the 7-Crowns Syndicate. Now, the weather posed the more immediate threat. They might not reach Flagstaff in one piece, much less Dallas where the trial was underway.

An hour ago, the snowstorm they'd been traveling through morphed into a blizzard the likes of which Kiera had never seen. According to her phone's news app, it was a rare weather anomaly created by the nearby mountains and an unexpected shift in air currents. That was the last she and Marshal Gifford learned before their phones lost reception and the car radio broadcast only static.

Kiera would be less nervous if Marshal Navarro had remained with them. They'd been forced to leave him at a hospital in Kingman when he suffered a pulmonary embolism. He'd claimed his shortness of breath was a symptom of increasing altitude, but then he'd developed a sharp pain in his chest. By the time they reached the hospital, he'd turned a disconcerting shade of blue.

The next closest US Marshals' office was in Flagstaff. Their choices had been to wait for another marshal to join them or drive to Flagstaff, two-plus hours away, and meet up with a marshal there. Driving had seemed the best option—until the blizzard hit.

"I can't believe there weren't any other vehicles on the road," Kiera said. Not that they'd have noticed. Visibility was practically zero.

"We were fortunate."

The understatement of the year. "How much farther to the junction?"

"About five miles. Best I can tell," the marshal added as she navigated a turn.

Best she could tell? For all Kiera knew, they were heading in the wrong direction. "I think we should turn around and go back to Kingman."

"We'll be past the storm soon."

Kiera had her doubts. Marshal Gifford was good at her job but no weather expert.

"Are you sure?" She pictured a warm comfortable, safe hotel room and desperately wanted to be there.

"According to that last weather report, it's supposed to be traveling southwest," Marshal Gifford said, as if that explained everything about a storm that had been inexplicable from the start.

"Can we stop in that town you mentioned? Wild Horse Pass? Wild Hills?" Kiera couldn't remember.

"Wild Wind Hills. And it's not a town, just a community with an RV park and a few dozen cabins."

Marshal Gifford didn't take her eyes off the road. It was then Kiera noticed the woman's white-knuckled grip on the steering wheel. Perhaps she wasn't as calm as she appeared. The thought caused a ripple of alarm to race through Kiera. She'd literally put her and her daughter's lives in the marshal's care. If the woman failed to protect them...

Kiera shoved the thought from her mind and checked again on Heather, now dozing. What she'd give for a single minute of her daughter's peace and tranquility. But Kiera's world had been only chaos and worry these last fifteen months since her husband's murder. The last two days had been a nightmare.

That was exactly the amount of notice she'd been given to pack and get ready for the trial. Then, this morning at 5:00 a.m. sharp, Marshals Gifford and Navarro had arrived on Kiera's doorstep in Fresno. They'd removed Kiera and Heather from her condo, a safe home provided by witness protection and, under the cover of darkness, hustled them into the waiting sedan.

"Maybe there's a gas station or restaurant where we can wait out the rest of the storm," she suggested. "I'm not sure we should be on the road."

"We have to keep moving. You know that."

Right. Moving objects were harder to hit.

Without her testimony, the 7-Crowns Syndicate's

second-in-command would walk. And, according to the US Marshal's office, the syndicate intended to guarantee the outcome by eliminating Kiera.

She adjusted Heather's blanket. "God will keep us safe."

Perhaps she should have left her daughter in Fresno. The Marshals' office had offered to provide a professional nanny and a twenty-four-hour security detail. Not only offered, they'd highly recommended.

But Kiera had refused. She couldn't bear the idea of being separated from Heather for a week or longer. Worse, what if the syndicate got to Heather while Kiera was in Dallas? She'd never forgive herself.

Then again, she'd never forgive herself if her daughter died in an accident en route to the trial.

"I need a break." Kiera straightened and rubbed her temples.

"There's a rest stop at the junction." Marshal Gifford's voice went uncharacteristically soft. "We can stay there for a little while."

"Thank you."

Kiera had only a moment to relax before another powerful gust of wind came out of nowhere. It sent them sailing across the ice as if riding on air. Kiera threw herself as much over the car seat as her seat belt harness would allow. Heather startled awake and squealed. Her blue eyes, inches from Kiera's, went wide as the car started spinning out of control.

Kiera screamed.

Marshal Gifford shouted, but in her fear and confusion, Kiera couldn't understand the words.

"Help us," she implored. To God, to the marshal, to her late husband, she wasn't sure.

Someone must have heard her because, bit by bit, the car slowed.

Kiera lifted her head, and her blood ran cold. They were still moving—no longer spinning, but in a straight line.

"Hold on," Marshal Gifford yelled an instant before they plowed headfirst into a snowbank that might as well have been made of bricks.

A deafening crunch followed, and the car shook from bumper to bumper. Kiera's head snapped violently forward, and her arms flew into the air. At the same time, the side airbag deployed, striking her shoulder and knocking her off balance. If not for the seat belt, she'd have ended up in the front seat. Or worse.

After that, her world went silent. Stars danced in front of her eyes. Her lungs seemed incapable of drawing a decent breath. A searing pain exploded at the base or her neck. But she was alive! Thank God.

Hearing her daughter's wails, she roused herself and let out an anguished cry of relief. Heather fussed and flailed, expressing her annoyance at what had just happened in typical baby-speak.

Ignoring her own pain, Kiera unbuckled her seat belt and buried her face in the blanket. Great sobs escaped her as she hugged Heather and the car seat to her chest.

"M-mommy's here, sweetie pie. I'm right h-here. Don't y-you fret."

"Kiera." Marshall Gifford spoke sharply from the front seat. "Are you okay?"

She collected herself and raised her gaze. "My neck hurts. What about you?"

"Nothing serious."

"Your face is bleeding."

Marshal Gifford rubbed a cut on her forehead, examined the small amount of blood and then wiped her fingers on her slacks. "I'll live." She tried starting the car. Nothing. Not even a disheartening click.

She grabbed her phone.

"Any reception?"

The marshal's answer was to grumble under her breath and toss the phone onto the front passenger seat.

"Looks like we're stuck for the time being," she said.

"What do we do?"

"Give me a minute to think."

Kiera fought to control her shaking. They couldn't go for help, not in this storm. And who knew their exact location? Kiera didn't. This Wild Wind Hills community could be miles away.

Then again, they were in danger just sitting here. It was freezing outside and would grow increasingly colder as night fell.

"The gas tank won't explode or anything?" Kiera asked, wondering if she'd watched too many action movies.

"I doubt it."

She wasn't reassured. "Is that a tree?"

"Yeah, buried in the snowbank. Must be what we hit."

It was then the acute hopelessness of their situation sank in. They were trapped. And it would be dark soon. "What's going to happen to us?"

"Don't panic."

How could she not? Even if Marshal Gifford managed to start the car, they weren't going anywhere. Not without a tow truck or a Good Samaritan. And unless the storm abated, neither was a possibility. While Marshal Gifford rummaged through the glove compartment and her travel bag, Kiera held a bottle of formula in her hands, attempting to warm it. Heather wasn't hungry, but Kiera needed something to occupy herself or she'd go crazy.

They were going be all right, she told herself over and over. God wouldn't abandon her and Heather, not after they'd come this far. He'd send help. She need only have faith.

Five minutes stretched into ten and then thirty.

"I see something!" Marshal Gifford pressed her face to the driver's side window.

Kiera stared, too, though her view was obstructed.

"There's a vehicle coming toward us."

Indeed, a silver shape materialized in the blinding snow. "It's a truck," Kiera said, her bones turning to jelly. They were going to be rescued.

"Stay quiet," Marshal Gifford ordered. "Let me do the talking." Dread filled Kiera as she realized her mistake. Rather than being rescued, they might be in grave peril. This could well be one of the 7-Crowns Syndicate's operatives sent to eliminate her.

"Remember our cover story."

Kiera swallowed. Cover story. Right. Think.

She silently reminded herself of the details and watched, with a mix of trepidation and excitement, as the truck came to a stop a few feet in front of them. The driver's side door opened, and a tall man emerged. He wore a bright blue winter parka and a cowboy hat sat on his head over a pair of earmuffs. He'd wound a red scarf around his neck, concealing his face from the eyes down.

Friend or foe? Kiera couldn't tell, and her pulse raced.

Suddenly, she saw it. The vivid green Christmas wreath with a big red bow affixed to the front of the truck.

Always a believer in signs, she was ready to accept that God had sent her one. This man, whoever he was, would rescue them.

Marshal Gifford was clearly less convinced and removed the Glock from her shoulder harness hidden beneath her jacket.

Clamping a hand to his cowboy hat, Nash Myers ducked into the wind and approached the disabled car. He had no business being out in a blizzard the likes of this one. The driver of the vehicle, even less. From the looks of the crumpled front end hugging the tree trunk, they might not have survived the crash had they been going any faster. Cheap auto store chains were no substitute for a good pair of snow tires and all-wheel drive.

Not to mention the requisite emergency supplies everyone should have. Nash carried an assortment in the back of his truck, including survival blankets and snowshoes. This person's trunk probably held reusable grocery bags.

Shielding his eyes from the frigid wind, he tried to make out the driver. A woman, mid-forties and with short blond hair, scrutinizing him with undisguised suspicion. Nash didn't blame her. He was a stranger, and she was traveling alone.

He pulled down the scarf covering his mouth and waved in greeting. When she didn't respond, he motioned for her to roll down the window. She did. A few inches.

"Are you okay?" he yelled.

She tilted her chin up to speak through the narrow opening. "A little banged up but fine."

"Have you been here long?"

"About an hour. Do you by chance have a tow rope in your truck?"

"I do, but even if I could pull you out, your car isn't going anywhere."

"What about a phone?"

"I tried calling the sheriff's office when I first spotted you. No reception."

"Is there a gas station around here?"

"Closest one's in Red Rock this side of the junction. I doubt they're open. Everyone's hunkered down inside to wait out the storm."

"A hotel?"

"Also in Red Rock."

Her jaw tightened.

Nash understood her frustration and fear. She was alone in a blizzard and had just lived through a harrowing crash. Now a stranger loomed outside her window.

"Look, my name is Nash Myers, and my family has a cabin over that hill," he said, attempting to convince her of his trustworthiness. He pointed in the direction of the cabin. "Everyone in Wild Wind Hills knows us."

"And your point?"

Not the response he'd expected. Most people in her circumstances would be glad assistance had arrived.

He tried again. "I realize you're scared, but you can't stay here. You'll freeze to death."

"The storm will clear soon."

"It won't. Not for another day or two."

"Are you sure?"

Before Nash could answer, a sudden movement in the back seat caught his attention. He bent and peered through the narrow open crack in the driver's side window. He'd been wrong about the driver traveling alone. A young woman in a purple stocking cap and puffy white coat occupied the rear seat. She hunched forward, her mittened hands clasped in front of her. He thought her teeth might be chattering.

What had possessed the pair of them to venture out on today of all days? He'd be at the cabin by now, sitting in front of a roaring fire, if not for the four-foot pile of snow blocking the road on his trip home from cutting a Christmas tree. It had taken him nearly an hour to shovel an opening through the snow wide enough for his truck.

Thank God. If the road had been clear, he might have passed this spot long before their accident and not been here to help.

"You have a blanket or an extra jacket we can use?" the driver asked. "And some water?"

"A blanket and water won't save you from hypothermia." Nash brushed away the film of ice crystals forming on his face. "You and your friend really need to come with me."

The driver shook her head.

"I get it. I'm a stranger, and you don't want to go off with someone who might turn out to be a serial killer."

She stiffened, and the woman in the back seat stifled a low cry.

"Hey, I'm joking," he quickly amended. "Relax, okay?"

They did. Marginally.

"Like I told you, everyone in these parts knows me." When neither responded, he tried a different approach. "We have a satellite dish at the cabin, so there's internet service. You can make Wi-Fi calls on your phone and send messages."

The woman in the back seat spoke for the first time. Her teeth were definitely chattering. "Our suitcases are in the trunk. Maybe if we put on extra clothing…"

"You can do that. But you'll spend a miserable few days and possibly suffer frostbite. Is that what you really want?"

"No." She hugged herself tight and shuddered, her glance darting to the seat beside her.

Why weren't the two of them sitting together to conserve body heat? They obviously knew zero about surviving in a blizzard. They hadn't even brought any water with them.

The driver suddenly shifted in her seat to face the younger woman, and a hushed conversation ensued. Whatever the two of them said to each other, Nash couldn't hear over the screeching wind.

Wait. Not the wind. A high-pitched wail came from inside the car.

He straightened, not quite believing his ears. "Is that a baby?"

The driver swiveled around, her expression as stormy as the sky above. "We decided we'd rather you went back to your cabin and sent help."

Was she kidding? "The nearest tow truck company is in Flagstaff, and the local sheriff's office won't come. They're stretched to capacity dealing with emergencies."

"*This* is an emergency."

"They may not see it that way. None of you are seriously injured. I'm also willing to transport you to safety."

"We have a baby."

"And I can't think of a better reason to get out of this blizzard."

The driver squared her shoulders.

Nash resisted the urge to pull on the handle and see if the door was locked. Were they truly so afraid of him they'd risk their lives and that of the baby's? Or were they hiding something?

Hard to tell, even for him. In his job as a compliance inspector for the Department of Agriculture, he frequently encountered people who were less than honest with him. He'd gotten good at reading faces and interpreting body language. These two, however, baffled him.

He imagined his mom and sister being in a similar situation and reined in his impatience.

In a calmer tone, he asked, "Could you live with yourself if that baby doesn't survive? Because I sure can't. Which is why I won't take no for an answer."

"We appreciate the offer—"

Nash cut her off. "There's hardly any visibility as it

is. If we don't leave now, this road will become a death-trap once the sun goes down."

"My toes are frozen solid," the younger woman said, more insistent now. "And I think Heather's lips might be turning blue."

Heather. The baby was a girl.

"How about this?" Nash proposed. "When we reach the cabin, the two of you go in first. I'll give you the Wi-Fi password, and you make your calls. Let your family or whoever know where you are. You can give them my name, phone number and the cabin address. Then, you can call the sheriff's office. Describe me to them. Give them my license plate number. They know me and will confirm my identity. I'll wait in the truck where you can keep an eye on me until you're done."

"What do you think, Marshal?" the younger woman asked.

Marshal? Nash frowned, certain he'd misheard. She must have said Marsha or Martha. The driver shot her a quelling look over her shoulder.

"Please," the young woman implored, a sob break-ing loose. "Heather is all I have. I can't lose her, too."

"What if he's…"

"What if he's not and the next person who comes along is?"

Marsha or Martha or whoever finally conceded with a reluctant nod. "As long as we go into the cabin first," she told Nash.

His muscles, tight from the cold and tension, loos-ened.

The younger woman instantly flew into action. She gathered a large bag, which she quickly stuffed with a few things from the seat. At the same time, the driver gathered her belongings and donned a navy blue cap with ear flaps. When she pressed a button on the dash and the trunk popped open, Nash almost missed noticing her placing a dark bulky object inside her jacket. A wallet, he guessed, though she went through a lot of effort to hide the object from his view.

A moment later, the younger woman emerged from the car.

"Step back," the driver yelled at Nash.

He did. She rolled up the window, shoved open the door and heaved herself out. Stumbling through the deep snow, she circled the car to join her companion.

By then, the young woman had picked up the baby in the car seat. Nash noticed she'd pulled a blanket up to cover the baby's face. Besides protecting her from the elements, it seemed to have quieted her crying.

The driver took hold of the young woman's arm in a possessive grip. "You bring the suitcases," she told Nash.

"Can do."

The driver immediately positioned herself between him and the young woman and watched as he went to the trunk. He moved slowly, not wanting to alarm her.

"I need the travel crib, too," the young woman said, pointing to a black canvas bag.

"Okay."

Once Nash had wrestled two wheeled suitcases and the travel crib out and onto the ground, he removed the red-knit scarf from his neck and laid it over the open trunk, letting the bottom two-thirds dangle in the air.

"What are you doing?" the driver demanded.

He pressed the button and shut the trunk, trapping the scarf. Not the best safety flag he'd seen, but it would suffice. "The snow will bury your car. This will alert anyone driving by to stay clear."

"There's a cross on it," the young woman said, her glance rising to meet his.

Nash's movements stilled. She had a small dimple in her chin and the bluest eyes he'd ever seen. The wariness she'd exhibited earlier had been replaced with interest.

"My mom makes scarves for locals in need and first responders," he found himself admitting. "She adds the cross to keep the wearer safe."

The young woman smiled. "That's nice."

Nash forgot about the snow and sleet pelting him and the chill penetrating him clear to his bones.

"Let's go." The driver's brusque order yanked him back to reality.

He motioned for the women to precede him.

"You first," the driver said.

He wasn't about to argue. She might panic and bolt.

Hoisting the strap on the travel crib over his shoulder, he grabbed the suitcase handles and started forward. The driver and young woman trailed a good six feet behind him.

As they trudged through the snow toward his truck, Nash thought again of the driver's peculiar actions. She could simply be overprotective, he reasoned. They were traveling with a baby, after all, and understandably scared.

He'd give her the benefit of the doubt. For now. Unless something happened to change his mind.

Chapter Two

Kiera drew up short when they reached their rescuer's truck. *Nash Myers.* She'd been silently repeating his name over and over—for safety reasons should she need to identify him. And she'd liked the sound of it. Of course, terrible people could have pleasant names. Take her late husband, for example.

"Is that a Christmas tree?" she asked, nodding at the truck bed.

As if discouraging any interaction, Marshal Gifford shifted to block Kiera's view.

"Yeah," Nash answered while loading the suitcases and travel crib alongside the tree. "I cut it down at Red Rock Butte. Which is why I happened by your car when I did."

"Can we save the chitchat for later?" Marshal Gifford groused.

Nash spared her a brief look before opening the rear passenger side door. Kiera tried to interpret his expression and couldn't. He may have been annoyed at the marshal's no-nonsense attitude. He may simply be in a hurry to get out of the blizzard.

"The rear seats are cramped." He gestured toward Kiera. "You and the baby might be more comfortable up front."

"I'll sit in the front," Marshal Gifford said.

Witnesses traveling under protection rode in the back seat. Nash had no idea of their situation, but Kiera knew from previous experience the marshal wouldn't bend.

"Suit yourself," he said.

Kiera was eager to put distance between herself and Nash. What could she do against a man like him if he proved to be sent by the syndicate? He stood at least six-two. And the impressive breadth of his shoulders wasn't due to his thick winter coat. If he wanted to, he could break her in half with little effort.

In another lifetime, someone of Nash's size and stature might have appealed to Kiera and made her feel safe. But she was leery. She could tell Marshal Gifford was, too, though she viewed *everyone* they encountered as a potential threat.

Holding the car seat with Heather close to her chest, Kiera gazed one last time at the Christmas tree before reaching for the open door. Cutting it down was either an incredibly crafted lie or the truth. And like the wreath on the front of the truck, she wanted to believe it was a sign from above.

Heeding her instincts had kept Kiera alive before, the night of her late husband's murder in particular. Still, she'd remain cautious of Nash. She was no fool. Especially when she had her precious daughter to protect.

He extended a hand as if to assist her with the car seat.

Marshal Gifford interceded. "She's fine. She can manage without your help."

Kiera could and would manage alone. She refused to entrust Heather with a complete stranger. She didn't even let Marshal Gifford, whose job it was to safeguard them, hold her baby.

Nash opened the rear passenger door. Setting the car seat with Heather inside, Kiera pushed it to the middle. Next, she dumped the diaper bag onto the floor and then climbed in. Once settled, she pulled down the blanket covering Heather's face.

Thank you, Lord! Her daughter's lips, while still tinged with blue, formed a gummy smile.

Kiera pressed a quick kiss to her daughter's forehead. "We'll be safe soon. I promise."

After securing the car seat, she fastened the seat belts, including hers. There wasn't much leg room, but she didn't care. Nash had left the truck running, and the warmth from the heater felt incredible. Her chilled toes and fingers tingled as blood resumed flowing to her extremities.

She didn't dare think they'd survived the crash only to land in the clutches of a 7-Crowns operative. Nash had to be one of the good guys. His mom knit scarves for first responders and people in need.

But Kiera had been betrayed before in the worst way by someone who'd vowed to love and cherish her. Why would a stranger be any different?

Marshal Gifford waited until Nash was walking around the front of the truck before getting in. "You okay?" she whispered to Kiera.

"Yes."

"Let me do the talking. And don't call me Marshal again. My name is Diane. Yours is Tara. Stick to our cover story."

"Right."

Kiera's cheeks heated with embarrassment, something not possible a few minutes ago in the icy cold. She knew better than to reveal their true identities. The importance of aliases had been drilled into her ever since she'd agreed to testify and entered the witness protection program. It was unlike her to slip up.

As was Marshal Gifford's uncharacteristic loss of composure. Kiera blamed the blizzard and accident. Both women were off their game, but they'd better get it together and fast. Their lives could depend on it.

"You might want to tone down the law enforcement attitude," Kiera said. "He could become suspicious and not buy our cover story."

The marshal opened her mouth, presumably to object, and then closed it. "You're right," she said.

Marshal Gifford was buckled in and facing forward by the time Nash settled into the driver's seat.

"All set?" he asked, removing a blue bandanna from his coat pocket and using it to wipe his damp face.

The marshal nodded. Kiera, too, when he glanced over his shoulder at her.

He had strong well-formed features. And large hands, which she noticed when he removed his gloves. His shoulders appeared even wider now in the truck. He seemed like someone who either worked outdoors or spent the bulk of his free time there. He'd cut down a Christmas tree by himself, hadn't he? That required some skill.

Did he have an axe? Was it in the truck bed? She hadn't thought of that and should tell Marshal Gifford.

Enough, she chided herself. She and the marshal were going into the cabin ahead of Nash. They'd make their calls and advise the US Marshals' office and Flagstaff Sheriff's Department of their location. Besides, if he meant to eliminate them, wouldn't he have done that at the car?

Kiera patted Heather and whispered a line from Psalm 4, a favorite that comforted her in times of distress.

"I will both lay me down in peace, and sleep. For thou, Lord, only makest me dwell in safety."

The psalm must have affected Heather as well for she quieted. Perhaps she sensed they were no longer in harm's way. Babies did pick up on people's moods and energy.

Nash eased the truck forward. It didn't slip and slide on the ice like the marshal's sedan. Kiera couldn't see the speedometer but guessed they were going ten miles an hour. Twelve at most. He wasn't taking any chances, which she appreciated.

"How far is your cabin?" Marshal Gifford asked.

"About a mile once we turn onto Cedar Circle Drive. It's around the next bend."

Kiera strained to see. Ice coated the window beside her, and the defroster had cleared only a small semicircle on the windshield.

Would she feel safer leaving the main road? They were less likely to be rescued if Nash proved to be working for 7-Crowns. Then again, they'd have been sitting ducks in their car if an operative came after them.

A flash of color appeared alongside the truck on the driver's side.

Marshal Gifford sat up even straighter. "What's that?"

Nash's answer was to tap the brakes to a stop and roll down his window. A blast of frigid air struck Kiera in the face.

"Bobby, hey! What are you doing out in this storm?"

A deep male voice carried on the wind. "Was going to ask you the same thing."

"I was heading home after cutting down Mom's tree, and I stopped to help these two ladies who went off the road. You'll see their car when you drive by. Do me a favor and make sure my safety flag is still visible."

"Will do."

"Be careful. It's nasty out here."

"If I don't see you before, Merry Christmas."

"Give my best to your family."

Nash rolled up his window. It wasn't until the man— Bobby—drove away that Kiera realized he was on a snowmobile.

She slowly relaxed. Nash *had* said he was known in these parts, and Bobby had called him by name. And if Nash had anything to hide, he would have kept quiet about the red scarf.

They started moving again. A few minutes later, Nash turned left, and they began an arduous climb up a single lane road.

So much for relaxing. Kiera tensed again. "You sure we won't slide down?"

"This is the worst part."

True to his word, the road became less steep. Kiera

admired Nash's skill driving under such extreme conditions. He must have considerable experience.

The strong-and-rugged type had always appealed to her. Which was why falling in love with and marrying a CPA had come as such a surprise to both her and her family. Joshua had been the most attentive suitor and devoted husband. A good provider, he'd sat beside her every Sunday at church and said grace along with her at every meal they shared. He'd donated money to charities and volunteered at the nearby food bank.

His deception had leveled her world. All the years Kiera had known him, he'd been leading a double life. Instead of heading off to the CPA firm where he'd supposedly worked, he'd been keeping the books for the 7-Crowns Syndicate.

He'd deceived them, too, and paid with his life when he got caught skimming. He'd nearly cost Kiera her life as well. Only by God's grace had she escaped unscathed.

"What were the two of you doing out in this blizzard?"

Nash's question jarred Kiera back to the present. She was safe, she reminded herself, and placed a hand on Heather. Please let them not end up trading one danger for another.

"We were on our way to our grandparents in Flagstaff," Marshal Gifford answered, her tone marginally less gruff.

"You're sisters?" Nash's brows rose in surprise.

"Cousins."

His glance met Kiera's in the rearview mirror, and she nodded.

"From Kingman?"

"Yes," the marshal said.

Nash didn't take his eyes off the road. "What are your names?"

"Tara," Kiera muttered.

"I'm Diane," the marshal said.

"Hmm." Nash appeared to digest that information.

Kiera's stomach knotted. Had he heard her say Marshal earlier?

"Lousy weather to be traveling in with a baby," he said after a moment.

"Is small talk a requirement—" The marshal stopped short, appearing to remember Kiera's warning. "Yes, it is. The blizzard came out of nowhere."

Nash gestured ahead. "Our cabin is next on the left."

Kiera hadn't spotted any other cabins through the snow. If anything, the blizzard was worse now. She couldn't see five feet out the window.

Suddenly, the truck jerked, and they started to climb again. Kiera automatically grabbed onto the handhold beside her and wrapped an arm around Heather's car seat.

"We're here," Nash announced.

She counted the passing seconds. How long was the driveway? Clearly, they weren't *here*. Not yet. She swallowed a gasp when the rear tires slid briefly before regaining traction.

"Hang tight," Nash said.

She did. Very tight. Her fingers hurt from clenching the handhold with all her might.

Through the swirling snow, a cabin took shape. Nash pulled beneath a carport and the snow abruptly stopped swirling. Kiera could see at last—thanks to the cover and a feeble exterior light. In front of them lay an enormous row of logs stacked three feet high. Tools hung from the wall. Snow shovels. Regular shovels. A rake. Gardening shears. An assortment of saws.

Makeshift weapons in the hands of the wrong person. Kiera remembered the likelihood of an axe in the truck that Nash had used to cut the Christmas tree.

The marshal already had her phone out and was tapping the screen. "Does the Wi-Fi signal reach out here?"

"It should," Nash said.

"What's your network called?"

"Myersnetlink."

The corners of the marshal's mouth turned down. "It isn't showing."

Nash retrieved his phone from the console cubby and tried. Kiera, too. She didn't find the network name, either.

"You said you had internet service," the marshal accused.

"We do have service. Since the power hasn't gone out, I'm guessing there's a problem with the satellite dish." He started to open his door. "Probably got knocked off balance by the wind. I'll have a look."

"You aren't leaving us alone," she said.

"Then come with me."

"We're not comfortable doing that without first making our calls."

Nash turned to look at the marshal. "I'm going to do my best to fix the problem. I suggest you head inside, dry off and make some hot coffee while you wait. Or remain here. One way or the other, you'll have to take your chances on me. I don't recommend heading out into that blizzard on foot."

"Can you drive us to a neighbor's house?" Kiera asked. "One with Wi-Fi?"

"I haven't met the new owner of the Wheeler place. He's the closest. The Carmichaels are gone for the entire month and their place is locked up. We can go door to door if that's what you want, though that will be difficult in this weather and with night falling. Wild Wind Hills isn't like the suburbs. Most houses are on three to five acres."

Kiera debated what to do. Before her husband's murder and learning of his deception, she would have accepted the kindness of strangers without hesitation, convinced most people were good and decent. Now, she questioned the motives of everyone she met.

All at once, Heather let out a loud I'm-starving wail. And she wouldn't stop until Kiera fed her something more substantial and appealing than a cold bottle of formula.

Nash and Marshal Gifford both sent Kiera inquiring looks. Nash's said the next move was up to her. The marshal's clearly transmitted Heather's timing could be better.

Heather's wailing escalated. *Please, Lord*, Kiera thought, closing he eyes, *help me make the right decision.*

The words spilled out before she realized it. "Is there a microwave in the cabin?"

As Nash neared the carport, the wind grabbed the aluminum extension ladder and tried to tear it from his hands. He struggled to hold on, convinced his arms might be pulled from their sockets.

Checking the satellite dish mounted on the front porch roof had been a complete waste of time as well as exhausting. The dish sat off-kilter and would require a technician to realign it. Anything Nash tried would only make matters worse. He'd lost his bandanna to the wind, watching it sail across the field separating his family's property from the Wheelers' old place. He was glad he'd traded his cowboy hat for a heavy woolen cap, also knit by his mom. If not, he'd have lost the cowboy hat, too.

Locking an arm around the ladder, he continued toward the carport, cold air blasting him in the face.

Nash couldn't remember a blizzard this strong. Thank God he'd found Diane and Tara and her baby. Bobby might not have noticed passengers in the car as he'd sped by on his snowmobile, and they might not have noticed him until it was too late to get his attention.

Inside the carport, Nash leaned the ladder against the tool wall next to the snow shovels. At least the firewood was dry. Should the power go out, they'd be able to stay warm and heat pans of food and water in the fireplace. The pipes potentially freezing was another problem he couldn't do anything about.

"I know you have a lot on your plate right now, God," he said as he brushed snow and ice from his coat, "what with everything there is happening in the world. But I think these two women might be in some kind of trouble. They and that baby in there could use some looking after. Along with everybody else affected by this blizzard." He stomped the excess moisture from his rubber boots before entering the mudroom. "I'm fine, by the way. You don't need to worry about me. Take care of those in need. And check in with my folks and sister, if you get a chance. Amen."

Removing his outwear, he toed off his rubber boots and replaced them with a pair of worn athletic shoes. Lastly, he donned a woolen vest over his plaid flannel shirt, his chilled insides needing the extra warmth.

When he entered the cabin's cozy kitchen, he discovered Tara sitting at the table. "Hey."

"Hello."

Her reserved gaze took him in from head to toe before she averted it. She'd propped her daughter in her lap and was entertaining her with a pink butterfly toy that played music. The baby loved the butterfly, if her giggles were any indication. A bottle of juice and half-empty jar of baby food sat on the table at Tara's elbow, a small spoon propped up in the jar.

"I made a pot of coffee." She tilted her head toward the counter. "There's plenty if you want a cup."

"I do, thanks." Nash went over to the coffeemaker and removed a mug from the rack. "It's cold out there."

"Any success with the satellite dish?"

"Naw. Fixing it is beyond my pay grade." After adding two spoonfuls of sugar to his coffee, Nash carried his mug to the large family-style table and sat in the chair next to Tara. "Afraid we're stuck with no internet for the duration. Sorry."

"I, um…"

Taking a sip of the rich brew, he peered at her over the rim of his mug. Alarm flashed in her eyes. The next second, she schooled her features into a blank slate.

"This blizzard won't last forever," he said.

"No." She shifted, increasing the distance between them by a slim margin.

Ah, thought Nash. He'd misread her alarm. She wasn't distressed by the loss of internet service but rather by his proximity.

He debated getting up and moving only to stay put. Throwing people off balance was a tactic he often used at work. They were more likely to reveal incriminating information if rattled—such as over-grazing by having too many cattle on their land or illegally diverting water onto their property.

Nash didn't consider himself the bad guy, though a lot of the people he investigated called him that to his face. He was protecting natural resources from abusers for the benefit of all.

"Where's Diane?" he asked.

"Looking around the cabin."

Looking around or inspecting every nook and cranny? Nash wouldn't put it past her. She must not have heard him come inside. Otherwise, she'd be here right now, her eyes trained on him. She'd dogged his heels when he'd carried the suitcases and travel crib upstairs and then back down the stairs when he was done. She'd watched him through the open mudroom door until he'd left to check on the satellite dish. Nash had half expected her to accompany him. Unsurprisingly, he'd glimpsed her in the living room window while he climbed the ladder.

Something was up with her, more than being hyperprotective of a younger cousin and small baby. Nash wouldn't jump to the conclusion they were criminals or kidnappers. Perhaps they were taking a large sum of money to their grandparents or Diane was helping Tara escape an abusive relationship. The explanation could be reasonable and one where Nash would want to help them.

"You two get settled in?"

"Yes," Tara said. "Thanks."

Nash had offered the women the two upstairs bedrooms, usually reserved for him and his sister and brother-in-law. He'd sleep in his parents' room tonight on the first floor. They'd have been here today if not for the blizzard. As it was, they were stuck in Flagstaff until the weather cleared.

The baby suddenly looked away from the butterfly and directly at Nash. Her small mouth spread into a wide smile.

Nash couldn't help himself and smiled in return. The kid was a cutie. Getting married and having a family was his eventual plan. He'd yet to meet that special someone, but at thirty-two, he figured he still had time. His mother was the impatient one. And while his sister would soon fulfil their fondest wish for a grandchild, she and her husband lived two states away.

"Heather looks content," he observed.

Tara nodded. "She's eaten and been changed. That generally improves her mood."

"My sister, Victoria, and her husband are having a baby."

"Really?"

"Yeah." Nash took another sip of coffee. "They were going to be here for Christmas. It's a Myers annual tradition. But her doctor recommended she stick close to home. Apparently, there's a chance she could go into early labor."

"Oh, dear. I'll say a prayer for her tonight."

The softly spoken remark touched Nash with its sincerity. Tara *would* say a prayer for his sister. She wasn't merely being polite.

Heather began to fuss and batted the butterfly away. Tara set down the toy and picked up the bottle of juice.

While the baby drank, Nash discreetly studied Tara. The mop of brown curls previously hidden beneath her purple hat surrounded her face in pretty disarray.

He liked her looks. He wouldn't lie. But they weren't what intrigued him most about her. Tara, same as her cousin Diane, was hiding something. Something that clearly unnerved, if not frightened, them. Yet, despite her small stature and reserved demeanor, Nash detected a strength in Tara lying just beneath her wary surface. He imagined it would be interesting to see her strength put to the test, if such a thing turned out to be necessary.

"When did you get back?"

Nash turned at Diane's voice. "A few minutes ago."

He assumed she'd sit on Tara's other side. Instead, she took the seat across from him.

"What's the status of the satellite dish?" she asked.

"The wind blew it sideways. There's nothing I can do."

Her jaw muscles worked. "You have a satellite radio?"

"No. And I don't know anyone who does."

"A two-way radio?"

"Nope." He shook his head. "We're going to have to wait for a break in the weather and cell phone service to resume."

"You'd think someone with a cabin in the remote mountains would be better prepared. Satellite dishes malfunction."

Nash refused to let Diane rile him. Lashing out was a reaction to stress, something they were all feeling.

"Wild Wind Hills isn't that remote, and blizzards like this are rare. We've only had a handful of problems since my parents bought the cabin."

"When was that?" Tara asked.

"Fifteen, no, sixteen years ago. The original owners were preppers and built the cabin right before Y2K. There are a half dozen secret cubbies and hidey-holes in the house and shed. There's an underground bunker the original owners supposedly stocked with enough supplies and water to last a year. Plus, gold coins. They were convinced the entire banking system would collapse."

"I noticed the trapdoor in the mudroom." Diane rose and poured herself a mug of coffee, not once taking her eyes off Nash.

Unlike her younger cousin, she was all hard corners and straight lines. Every move she made, even something as mundane as pouring coffee, was executed with purpose and precision. While Tara's strength came from within, Diane could probably bend nails with her bare hands.

"The trapdoor leads to the bunker," Nash said. "It's mostly empty now except for some old folding chairs and a table. There's a toilet, sink and shower that still work."

Tara grimaced. "Must be cold and damp down there."

"Cold, yes. Not damp. The previous owners built a state of the art ventilation system. My parents used to store stuff down there, but mom started having trouble with the steps. They use the cubbies off the upstairs bedrooms now."

"Where do you live?" Diane asked.

Despite her effort to pose the question casually, Nash sensed she was digging for information.

"Camp Verde. I come here at least once a month. Mostly with my family. Sometimes my college buddies join me for a fishing weekend."

"Where do you work?"

"The Department of Agriculture. I'm a compliance inspector. My parents live in Phoenix, though they were in Tucson this past week at the U of A College of Medicine."

"Are they medical professionals?"

"They were there seeing a new doctor and exploring possible treatment plans. My mom has multiple sclerosis."

Tara's expression filled with sympathy. "I'm so sorry."

Nash attempted to suppress the pang that always accompanied any discussion of his mom's disease. "She was doing fairly well, but it's been tough lately. Dad retired early to become her full-time caregiver. I help out as much as I can."

"I'm sure they appreciate that."

"It's getting late," he said and pushed his chair back from the table. "Anyone hungry? I'm not much of a cook, but there's some canned stew in the pantry and a box of corn bread mix."

He expected at least one of them to offer to pitch in. Instead, they remained seated. All right.

The wind outside picked up and a tree branch slammed against the darkened kitchen window, making a loud noise. Tara gasped and pulled the baby close to her. Diane spun in her seat and shoved her hand inside her jacket. At the last second, she froze.

"It's okay," she murmured to Tara, slowly withdrawing her hand. "It's just the wind."

Tara nodded, grim-faced.

Nash stared, alarm bells going off in his head. Something told him he'd been wrong earlier about not jumping to conclusions. He'd seen enough people reaching for a gun to know that was exactly what Diane was doing.

Chapter Three

Kiera patted her daughter's back as she paced the bedroom. "Shh, sweetie pie. Don't cry."

Heather had initially fallen asleep only to wake up an hour later. Despite Kiera's many attempts, Heather had progressed from mild complaining to a full-blown crying fit. Overtired, no doubt, and agitated from the unusual day and strange surroundings. Just like her mom. Kiera wouldn't mind indulging in a little crying fit of her own to release her pent-up tension.

It was just past nine o'clock. She and the marshal had retired to their separate bedrooms after the simple dinner Nash prepared. During a short *briefing*, as the marshal referred to their talks, she and Kiera had both agreed Nash appeared to be who and what he claimed. Nonetheless, they'd remain vigilant. The marshal had instructed Kiera to not only lock her door but wedge a chair beneath the doorknob for added security. Together, they'd shoved a bookcase several feet to the left, blocking the window. A 7-Crowns operative would be able to breach the barriers, but not without making a ruckus, giving Kiera and the marshal advance warning.

She felt marginally safer, though between her humming nerves and Heather's crankiness, any sleep was doubtful.

Kiera had been surprised when the marshal didn't insist they share a bedroom. It was possible she trusted Nash more than she let on. Or she hadn't wished to interfere with Kiera and Heather's routine. More likely, she'd chosen to distance herself from a fussy baby. Kiera still didn't know if the marshal had children of her own after all the time they'd spent together. She hadn't revealed any personal information of *any* kind and didn't wear a wedding ring. If not for those rare moments when she looked at Kiera with a hint of compassion in her steely eyes, she might have been a robot.

Heather's crying escalated. Kiera had tried a bottle, applesauce, burping, an array of toys, warmer pajamas, cooler pajamas, rocking Heather in her arms, singing lullabies, playing white noise on her phone and gentle massage. Nothing worked.

No doubt Kiera's stress added to Heather's crankiness. She couldn't help worrying about the trial. They were already late at this point. Would it be postponed? Ruled a mistrial? She'd hate for that to happen after all she'd gone through.

Heather let out another loud wail.

"What would I do at home?" Kiera asked herself.

The answer was easy. She'd take Heather for a ride through the neighborhood. Or they'd lie in the hammock in the backyard. A change of scenery combined with motion usually quieted Heather. But seeing as neither option was available…

Kiera could go downstairs. Earlier, she'd spotted a rocking chair in the living room.

No, Marshal Gifford would have a fit. But Nash had mentioned retiring early. Kiera would be alone.

Okay. Bad idea. And asking for trouble.

Poor little Heather began to hiccup, and her face bloomed a vivid red. Kiera was becoming less worried about waking the entire household and more concerned about her baby. Twice before, she'd cried so hard she threw up. Kiera had to do something.

She shoved her hair off her face with her free hand and glanced around the room, seeking inspiration. In that instant, she decided. She'd step into the hall, and if Marshal Gifford didn't emerge from the bedroom next door to stop her, Kiera would take Heather downstairs. After removing the chair from beneath the doorknob, she gave Heather a pacifier and grabbed a bottle just in case.

Two minutes later, she was creeping down the carpeted steps, Heather tucked against her side. Already, Heather's distress had lessened.

At the entrance to the living room, Kiera paused. It was as if the comfortable accommodations beckoned her. A lit lamp sitting on an end table beside the sofa glowed softly. An afghan—probably knit by Nash's mom—lay neatly over the sofa arm. An antique wall clock ticked quietly, its brass pendulum counting the seconds. A collection of photos lined the fireplace mantel. The spicy scent of cedar reminded Kiera of her parents' home during the holidays and the chest where her mom stored Christmas linens.

Tears sprang to her eyes as she lowered herself into the padded rocking chair. She'd spoken to her family only twice since entering witness protection and she missed them so much. Heather had met none of her grandparents, aunts, uncles and cousins in person and wouldn't until after Kiera testified. If then. Everything depended on the trial's outcome. If her husband's murderer was found guilty and the 7-Crowns sought revenge against her for testifying, Kiera would have no choice but to live out the remainder of her life in witness protection.

She was often tempted to contact her parents on her own. The Marshals' office had adamantly warned her against such a dangerous move, and Kiera had followed their directive. She'd never put her family in jeopardy. It was possible, especially now, that the 7-Crowns Syndicate kept close tabs on her parents as a means of finding Kiera.

Releasing a sigh, she pushed rhythmically with her foot. The rocking chair's motion had a calming effect on Heather. Thankfully. Kiera found herself mentally reviewing the day's events, starting when the marshals arrived at her condo, Marshal Navarro's pulmonary embolism and their stop at the Kingman hospital, the car crash and Nash rescuing them. Despite her growing confidence that he intended no harm, she could still be found by a 7-Crowns operative even in Wild Wind Hills and during a blizzard.

On a whim, she tried her phone again. She and the

marshal had been checking at least every hour. So far, no bars and no service alerts. Now was no different.

At the sound of a door opening in the kitchen, Kiera sat bolt upright, her blood running cold. Heather roused and whimpered.

Next, came a door closing and the rustling of…what in the world? Kiera pushed to her feet, ready to flee.

If she ran upstairs, she'd have no means of escape, but the marshal was there with her gun.

"Oh, for crying out loud," a low male voice grumbled.

Was that Nash? The rustling sound continued only to stop when something landed on the floor with a clatter.

"Give me a break," he complained.

It *was* Nash.

Kiera bolstered her courage and started toward the kitchen. If he had plans to kill her, he was sure being noisy about it. She came upon him lugging his Christmas tree through the kitchen. A chair lay on its side, toppled by a branch.

"What are you doing?" Kiera blurted without thinking.

Nash paused and straightened, one hand supporting the tree. "Sorry if I woke you."

"You didn't. I was up." She studied him and the tree. "Can I help?"

"I should have moved the chairs first."

A self-effacing smile tugged at the corners of his mouth. It altered everything about his features, turning him from strong and imposing to friendly and, yes, charming. Kiera felt an unexpected fluttering in her tummy and not from nerves or fear.

Her reaction startled her, and she retreated a step, refusing to label her response to him as attraction.

"I...um..."

"Can you pull the chair out of the way?" he asked, appearing unaware of her discomposure. "I can't reach around the tree."

"Sure." She could hardly refuse.

Balancing Heather on her hip, Kiera bent and grabbed the chair, tugging it clear and setting it upright. Without Nash asking, she moved the neighboring chair as well, creating a pathway.

"Thanks."

He carried the tree into the living room. Kiera followed, her curiosity getting the better of her. He placed the tree near the window in a stand she hadn't noticed before.

"I had trouble sleeping," he said as he knelt and tightened the screws that held the tree trunk in place. "Figured I should do something productive. Get this beast set up and watered. I was trying to be quiet."

Which explained why Kiera hadn't heard him before she came downstairs. "I had trouble sleeping, too. And so did Heather." She moved the baby to her other side. "It's been a long day."

He stepped back and evaluated the tree. "Look balanced to you?"

When was the last time Kiera had set up a Christmas tree? Her mind ventured to her and Joshua's first Christmas together as husband and wife. They'd delighted in stringing the lights and placing the ornaments, laughing and teasing each other and dreaming about what the future held.

Pain squeezed her heart. Lies. Their entire life together

had been one big lie, from the moment they met through mutual friends. What she'd give to change the past.

"Kiera?" Nash asked.

His question returned her to the present. "Yeah. The tree's balanced. Though, I'd turn that bare spot to the back."

He did as she instructed and then nodded with satisfaction. "Much better."

They stood there, gazing at each other, the moment stretching to the point of awkwardness.

"Well, Heather's getting sleepy again," Kiera said. "I'll see you in the morning."

"Wait. I was going to make a cup of hot chocolate. You want one to take upstairs with you?"

"Yeah. I'd like that." She smiled at him for the first time tonight.

"I'll be right back."

"Okay."

Once he'd gone, she sat back down in the rocking chair, wondering if she'd lost her mind and if it was too late to escape to her room. Heather promptly dozed off, nestled in the crook of Kiera's arm. From the kitchen, she could hear Nash rearranging the chairs and the clanging of a pan. Soon, he reappeared with two steaming mugs.

That, Kiera supposed, was her cue to rise and take her hot chocolate upstairs. Only she didn't. Instead, she remained seated, extended a hand and accepted the mug Nash offered. At her murmured, "Thank you," he set his mug on the coffee table and lowered himself onto the couch. She had invited him to join her, after all, by not leaving.

"I came up a day early this year to cut the tree and put up the decorations before my folks got here."

"To surprise them?" Kiera sipped her hot chocolate. It was delicious.

"Not exactly. Mom loves to decorate the cabin. But it's getting harder and harder for her, what with her multiple sclerosis. I knew if I didn't have everything done when she got here, she'd overdo it and then be too miserable and hurting to enjoy Christmas."

"That's very sweet of you."

"The blizzard came in like gangbusters while I was cutting down the tree. I wasn't sure I'd make it home."

"Speaking for me and Heather and…my cousin, we're very glad you came by when you did."

"If you don't mind me saying, you two don't look related."

Kiera swallowed, forcing herself to remain calm. Nash was no dummy and paid close attention. He'd notice her distress. "No, I guess we don't."

"Are you close?"

"We could be closer. This is our second trip together." Not a lie. The marshal had originally escorted Kiera to her condo in Fresno.

Whenever possible, she stuck close to the truth. Less chance of slipping up that way and contradicting herself later on.

Nash sipped his hot chocolate in contemplative silence. Kiera waited. But all hope the topic of Marshal Gifford had exhausted itself was dashed by his next remark.

"She seems a little high-strung."

"She can be."

"Is she by chance in law enforcement?"

"Um," Kiera faltered. "She's former military."

"That would have been my next guess."

She released a breath, her mental wheels turning. She needed to provide Nash with a plausible excuse for the marshal's overprotectiveness and no-nonsense demeanor. If not, he'd start asking questions. Questions they weren't prepared to answer. "She's been very protective of me since my husband passed suddenly last year."

Nash's expression sobered. "I'm very sorry for your loss."

"I appreciate that. Things haven't been easy for me, and I've come to rely on…Diane a lot."

"It's good you have someone."

"I trust her more than anyone." Definitely not a lie. "There's nothing she wouldn't do for me."

Nash worked his jaw as if to ask another question. Kiera tensed, ready to recite her list of rehearsed answers about what she did for a living, how her husband had died and where her pretend parents lived in Flagstaff.

"The decorations are in the cubby off your bedroom," Nash said. "I'll need to get in there tomorrow morning. Whenever's convenient for you."

Whew. He wasn't going to grill her. The knot between Kiera's shoulders eased. "Absolutely."

He drained the last of his hot chocolate and rose. "It's getting late. Think I'll call it a night."

Kiera also stood, careful not to jostle Heather and wake her. "Let me rinse out these mugs."

"I'll do it. You have your hands full."

"Thanks again…Nash." She relinquished her empty mug.

"Sleep well."

His smile ignited a small spark. Kiera instantly chastised herself. Even if her wounded heart could learn to love again in the wake of Joshua's betrayal, she was in no position to form a romantic attachment. Certainly not as long as she remained in witness protection. And who knew how long that would be?

"Good night." Kiera padded out of the living room toward the stairs. The last thing she heard was water running in the kitchen sink.

A small part of her had longed to remain. She hadn't sat and casually conversed with anyone in ages. The reminder of her old life left her feeling lonely and melancholy.

When she reached the top of the stairs, the marshal's door flew open, and she stopped short. For several seconds, they stared at each other, Kiera's pulse hammering.

"Were you in the bathroom?" the marshal asked in a loud whisper, her eyes puffy as if she'd just awoken.

Kiera hesitated. "Just heading there now."

"You try your phone again?"

"I did a while ago." Before running into Nash and drinking hot chocolate. "No service."

"Heather's finally asleep, I see." The marshal glanced at the baby in Kiera's arms.

"Yes. I should get her to bed."

"Right. You be careful."

Kiera ducked into her room. Closing the door, she leaned her back against it, Heather cradled to her chest. Too late, she remembered she'd not gone to the bathroom.

Why hadn't she told Marshal Gifford about Nash?

Was she afraid of being subjected to another lecture on safety and precautions?

Even as the thought occurred to her, Kiera recognized it as untrue. She wanted that moment with Nash to remain between the two of them.

The question was why? Kiera had never kept secrets from the marshal. Especially secrets as risky as a private conversation with a virtual stranger.

Nash opened the refrigerator door and surveyed the contents. "You okay with eggs, toast and orange juice?"

"You can't keep cooking for us," Tara insisted.

She sat at the table, knee to knee with Heather, who was secured in a portable baby seat buckled to the chair. Tara had produced the cloth contraption from a bulging diaper bag that appeared to contain enough baby supplies for a week. The preppers who'd once owned this cabin could take a lesson in packing techniques from her.

"Little else to do around here." He glanced over his shoulder at the window, the same window the tree branch had smashed against the previous night. "Not until the weather breaks."

"I refuse to let you wait on us."

Tara spooned another bite of awful looking oatmeal mush into Heather's mouth. The baby clearly had undiscriminating taste, for she ate hungrily. Nash grimaced and returned to the open refrigerator.

"Hope you like your eggs scrambled."

"Please don't go to any trouble."

"Too late."

He removed a full carton of eggs and set it on the

counter. He added a tub of butter, a loaf of bread and a jug of orange juice. Nash had brought only a single ice chest of perishables with him, counting on his parents to supply the remaining food for their extended holiday stay. No chance of starving, though, since the pantry was stocked with plenty of canned and dry goods.

"I'll wash the dishes," Tara offered, using the spoon to scrape oatmeal from Heather's chin.

Was that really how people fed babies? Nash needed to have a long talk with his neatnik sister. She should be told.

From the living room came the sound of furniture being moved. Since coming downstairs that morning, Diane had been trying every possible location in the cabin to test her phone's reception, including the front and back porches. So far, she'd struck out. Considering the way the blizzard continued to dump snow on them, Nash doubted she'd have any success.

"How about you make the toast?" he suggested to Tara. "When you're done feeding Heather."

"She's had plenty for now. I might give her a bite or two of my eggs."

Tara rose and rolled her slim shoulders as if they ached. After double-checking the baby-seat straps and giving her daughter a toy, she came over to stand beside Nash.

"The toaster's next to the can opener." He cracked an egg into a mixing bowl. "Under that flowered cover."

"Your mom make this, too?" She lifted off the cover.

"She's into crafts."

"And very talented."

"I think she single-handedly raised five hundred dollars in donations for the last annual church bazaar."

They exchanged smiles. Nash wanted to ask Tara if she'd told her cousin about their conversation last night, but he refrained. They were growing comfortable together. A vast improvement from yesterday. Calling attention to that might alter the atmosphere between them.

The small kitchen wasn't designed for two people. Nash and Tara bumped elbows, stepped on toes and murmured, "Oops, sorry," more than once.

"I'm used to cooking alone," he explained.

"Me, too," Tara admitted. After a long pause, she added, "Joshua worked long hours. I did most of the cooking."

"What did he do for a living?"

She hesitated again, for several seconds longer this time. "He was a CPA for a large accounting firm."

Her answer struck him as rehearsed. Especially when she didn't elaborate on how her husband died. He also didn't believe her cousin Diane was former military. She'd reached for a concealed weapon last night, and whether she'd actually been carrying one or not, Nash wasn't certain.

Then again, she might be former military and currently employed in private security. Which implied Tara was a high profile individual. She didn't look or act like a celebrity, and her face wasn't familiar to him. But Nash only perused the headlines and paid no attention to Hollywood gossip. She could be a politician's daughter traveling incognito because of threats to her publicly prominent parent, and he'd have no idea.

"What about you?" Nash asked. "You work?" He tried to sound casual rather than itching with curiosity.

"I'm an insurance claims processor and get to work from home. Which is great because I don't have to put Heather in day care. The hours are flexible, too, as long as I get my forty in every week."

So, she wasn't an heiress or a celebrity. "It's nice the company accommodates you."

"They're not entirely selfless," she said. "Having employees telecommunicating saves them money."

"Do you ever tire of the solitude? I couldn't work from home. I need to breathe fresh air. Talk to people. Otherwise, I'd go stir-crazy."

"Heather keeps me pretty busy. Though once she starts walking, I'll have trouble getting my job done. You should see how fast she can crawl when she puts her mind to it. And she's into everything. I can't turn my back on her for a second. She once emptied an entire bottle of lotion onto her crib mattress. Smeared it all over herself in the process." Tara rolled her eyes at the memory.

This was the most she'd spoken since she and Nash had met. And while nothing she'd said was particularly revealing, it rang true. He also liked that she trusted him enough to open up, even if it was just about mundane stuff.

Tara was buttering the last piece of toast and Nash portioning scrambled eggs onto plates when Diane entered the kitchen.

She took one look at them and asked, "What's going on?"

Nash sensed Tara's tension, though she had nothing

to feel guilty about. However, if she was running from an abusive man, Diane may not like the idea of Tara being alone with Nash.

He pointed to the three glasses he'd filled while the eggs were cooking. "Grab yourself some orange juice, Diane. Breakfast is ready."

"Tara." She drew out her cousin's name.

"I'm helping Nash." Tara's words tumbled from her mouth in a rush. "And you and I are cleaning the kitchen after breakfast. He's done enough for us."

Diane's eyes remained glued to Tara and Nash as she grabbed a glass off the counter and one of the plates. Evidently, hunger won out over determination.

When they were all seated and digging into their food, Diane asked Nash, "Will you be checking on the satellite dish again?"

"I wasn't planning to. Not with this wind."

"Can we try a neighbor? They must have Wi-Fi."

Boy, she didn't give up. Nash couldn't remember meeting a more stubborn individual. "I doubt the roads are drivable. I won't risk getting my truck stuck in snow and having to walk back on foot."

"But you have all-wheel-drive."

"The snow's already past my knees. Higher in some places. At the rate it's falling, we may not make it down the driveway, much less to a neighbor's house a quarter mile away." He finished the last of his eggs. "There's a snowmobile in the shed."

That clearly piqued Diane's interest. "We can take that."

"It carries two people. Which one of you is going

to stay behind with the baby? Unless you want me to go alone."

Her mouth flattened. "No."

He hadn't thought so.

"Can you teach me to drive it?" She shot Tara a glance. "We could take the baby with us. Tuck her inside your coat."

Tara drew back in alarm. "I don't like that idea."

Nash turned to Diane. "I'm not sending an inexperienced snowmobile driver out in this blizzard. Visibility is terrible. And if you run into a log or ditch buried beneath the snow, you'll flip and injure yourselves. Or worse."

Tara put a hand on Heather's leg.

His harsh warning did the trick and quieted Diane for the remainder of the meal. Tara, too. Heather was the only one making noise as she smacked her lips whenever Tara gave her a small bite of scrambled eggs.

When the two women started clearing dirty dishes, Nash pushed back from the table.

"I'm going to head upstairs and get the Christmas decorations out of the cubby in Tara's room."

Diane instantly tossed the dishcloth she'd been holding onto the counter. "I'll come with you."

"That's not necessary."

"You stay here," she told Tara.

"I don't have a two-way radio or .22 rifle hidden in the cubby."

"I'll come with you," Diane repeated and stared him down.

After a moment, Nash caved. "Okay. You can help

me carry boxes." If she was going to track his every move, he'd at least put her to work.

Upstairs, he entered the first bedroom. The travel crib had been set up alongside the bed, a pink blanket draped neatly over the side. Tara's closed suitcase lay on the floor near the crib. Heather's baby items were nestled together atop the freshly made bed. Tara was quite tidy, or a very considerate houseguest.

"The cubby's over here." He made straight for the far corner of the room where he dragged a straight-back chair out of the way.

To the casual eye, the cubby was invisible, its four-by-three-foot door covered with the same wood paneling as the walls. Nash pressed a recessed button that resembled a knot in the wood paneling, and the door drifted open several inches.

"Clever," Diane commented. She stood behind him. *Close* behind him.

"Like I said, the original owners were serious preppers. And possibly a little paranoid."

He had to stoop over in order to enter the cubby. Inside, he waved his hand in the air until his fingers brushed against a string dangling from the ceiling, which he then pulled to turn on a single bare light bulb. The yellow glow from its forty-watts cast an eerie glow over the cubby's contents.

Crammed full of boxes, bins, bags and totes, there wasn't much room for Nash to maneuver. As kids, he and his sister, Victoria, had played spy and tomb explorer and rocket ship in this small space. The bunker in the basement had been their clubhouse. One summer, they and their dad had spent an entire weekend re-excavating the abandoned underground tunnel leading from the bunker to the shed, celebrating triumphantly when they were able to successfully crawl from one end to the other. That same year, Nash received a pair of walkie-talkies for Christmas. Victoria would hide in the other cubby next door, and she and Nash would talk for hours. They'd even developed their own code.

He tugged the first box off the stack and walked backward into the bedroom. There, he set it down. "How much can you carry?" he asked Diane.

"More than that."

Altogether, they made three trips downstairs, setting the decorations in the middle of the living room. By then, Tara had finished in the kitchen. She'd placed Heather on a blanket in front of the couch, but the baby was determined to investigate her surroundings on all fours and refused to stay put, leading Tara on a merry chase.

"Where do we start?" Tara asked, capturing Heather and swinging her up into her arms.

"The lights are always tangled," Nash said. "I don't know how that happens." He opened the lid on a plastic tote, revealing a bundle of tree lights.

While they sorted and came up with a game plan, Diane glanced over her shoulder toward the stairs. "There's something I forgot. Be right back."

Nash stared after her retreating back, then exchanged glances with Tara, who answered with a shrug. Diane was voluntarily leaving them alone? That was an interesting change.

Ten minutes later, Diane still hadn't returned. Also interesting. And, perhaps, concerning.

Nash sorted through the remaining boxes. "The nativity scene's missing. I'm going after it." The heirloom set, which had belonged to Nash's grandmother, was his mom's favorite.

Tara had untangled the lights and was stretching them out in a long row. She managed to keep Heather from interfering by letting the baby play with a stuffed elf.

As Nash neared the top of the stairs, he realized from the closed bathroom door that Diane was inside and slowed his steps to quietly pass, not wanting to disturb her. Inside the cubby, he retrieved the box containing the nativity scene from a shelf. Behind it, he discovered another box, this one containing battery-operated candles. He tested one, then another, and gave a chuckle when they lit.

"They're not kidding when they say long-lasting batteries."

Before leaving the bedroom, he put two of the candles in the window. Light sensitive, they would automatically come on at night. His mom always liked the way the candles looked from a distance. She thought they gave the cabin a welcoming holiday air.

Nash dug though the box and located another working pair, which he put in the window of the second bedroom. One box under each arm, he reentered the hall. He came to a halt when he heard Diane's muffled voice from behind the closed bathroom door.

He stopped and listened. Had she finally gotten service on her phone? If so, why hadn't she hollered downstairs for Tara to join her? Fishing his phone from his jeans pocket, he looked at the display. One bar appeared only to immediately vanish.

Diane must be faring better than him. He thought about calling to Tara but hesitated. Leaning closer, he strained to hear Diane.

"Be careful," he swore he heard her say. "I'll call again when I can. In the meantime, trust no one. I love you. Bye."

Nash had only two seconds to process what he'd heard when the door suddenly flew open and Diane emerged. She took one look at him and stopped short, her eyes filling with guilt and alarm.

She blinked and covered her reaction with a display of bravado. "What are you doing here?"

"I was about to ask the same question."

"I…was trying for service. I stood on tiptoes and held my phone out the window."

On closer examination, Nash realized the ends of her short hair were damp, along with her cheeks.

"It can happen if the clouds shift."

She blew out a breath. "I never got through."

Except she *had* gotten through long enough to leave what sounded like a message.

Rather than accuse her of lying—she'd only deny it, anyway—he gestured to the box in the crook of his arm. "I'd better get this downstairs."

He could feel Diane's eyes boring into him as they went downstairs. She knew he'd heard her leaving a message. The question was what was she going to do about it? Confess to Tara or wait and see if Nash did?

Chapter Four

Kiera sat cross-legged on the living room floor, surrounded by an assortment of ornaments. Ever since the marshal and Nash had reappeared with the antique nativity scene, the pair had been eyeing each other from opposite ends of the room. Something had clearly transpired between them. Neither had said anything to Kiera, nor had they tried to get her alone to divulge the details. Still, she was certain.

How long would this weird standoff of theirs last? The small hands on the antique clock approached ten. If the marshal didn't confide in Kiera by noon, she was going to confront her and demand an answer.

Heather had tired of the elf and was now lying on her side, attempting to stuff her socked foot into her mouth. She'd fall asleep soon, and then Kiera would cover her with the afghan and let her nap where she lay. The trip upstairs to the travel crib would wake her, and Kiera wanted to avoid that if at all possible. Besides, Heather's morning naps were generally short, unlike her afternoon ones.

Kiera found it hard to believe, watching her little baby playing happily, that she'd been such a terror last night. Nothing like a good night's rest to improve one's mood. If only Kiera could say the same for herself. By her calculations, she'd managed at most four hours of hit-or-miss sleep.

But a nap of her own was out of the question. Between the trial, the blizzard, the constant threat of being targeted and Nash, her thoughts refused to stop spinning.

"Do you think those are any good?" She pointed to a box of plastic-wrapped peppermint candy canes clearly leftover from a previous year.

Nash poked his head out from behind the tree and the lights he was stringing. "Does anyone really eat those?"

"I'll put them in a dish on the coffee table." She resumed sorting the ornaments.

Marshall Gifford perched stiffly in the rocking chair Kiera had occupied the previous night, sipping her third cup of coffee. She probably wouldn't nap, either.

Outside, the wind howled. Each time it rattled the windows, the marshal would startle anew and twist in the chair.

"I noticed some snowshoes hanging in the shed outside," she said.

"Yeah," Nash mumbled as he replaced a burned out bulb.

"We could take those with us later when we drive to the neighbors'. In case the truck gets stuck."

Kiera groaned. They weren't seriously talking about this again, were they? She knew the marshal only wanted to report their location and get them back on the road. But enough was enough. Kiera absolutely refused to endanger her baby daughter. Not with the blizzard continuing to rage.

"There are only two pairs," Nash said, abandoning the lights to study the marshal. "Who's going to stay behind in the truck while the other two go for help?"

"You're assuming we'll get stuck."

"Have you looked outside lately?" His tone held a slight edge.

"We can't just sit here," the marshal bit out.

"Will you please stop arguing?" Kiera squeezed her eyes shut. "I'm not taking Heather into this blizzard, and I'm not staying alone with her."

For a long moment, they were all silent.

"I understand your impatience," Nash finally said, addressing the marshal. "I'm impatient, too. But the fact is we're stuck here for the duration. The good news is we have shelter and plenty of food. Why take chances? Will another day make any difference? You're only going to a family Christmas."

But they weren't. Kiera was supposed to be testifying in two days and spending the entire day tomorrow preparing with the prosecution.

Nash and the marshal engaged in a battle of heated stares. Kiera swore something challenging flashed in his dark brown eyes. No, not that. Accusatory. But of what?

The marshal visibly tensed. Kiera noticed. Nash, too, she was certain.

What was going on with them? Kiera almost asked only to change her mind, afraid she'd further antagonize them.

"Do you need help with the lights, Nash?"

Had she called him by name before? If yes, she couldn't remember. She had spoken his name to Marshal Gifford, but that wasn't the same. The ease with which it had rolled off her tongue surprised her. She'd apparently lost her caution around him—which might not be a good thing. Kiera couldn't afford to be distracted or grow complacent.

"Thanks," he said. "I can manage."

Probably for the best.

Nash finished with the lights and then put the tree topper on, an exquisite golden star with little bulbs in the center and on each point.

"All right," he announced to the room in general. "Let's see if this works."

He inserted the plug into an outlet, and the tree burst to life in a multitude of colors. The star glowed white, the perfect final touch.

"It's beautiful," Kiera exclaimed, her throat closing as emotions overwhelmed her.

Last Christmas, she hadn't bothered to buy holiday cookies or put so much as a wreath on her door. She'd been homesick and sad and feeling the effects of her unexpected pregnancy. She'd had no idea she was having a baby until after she moved to Fresno, attributing her symptoms to grief and shock.

This Christmas would be a repeat of last year's, only she'd have exhaustion and stress from the trial to add to her depression. Their time here at Nash's cabin, which would end soon, was the closest she'd come to celebrating Christmas. She couldn't wait to put ornaments on the tree. Later, when no one was looking, she'd take pictures with her phone, including the nativity scene. She'd already captured a video of Heather playing with the elf.

"Look, sweetie. Isn't it pretty?"

When she went to lift her daughter and show her the tree, she discovered Heather had drifted off to sleep. Kiera reached behind her for the afghan and covered Heather, smiling when she stuck her little thumb in her mouth.

"I think we should start with the homemade ornaments," she said to Nash and held up a red bulb with a snow scene on it. "Did your mom paint this?"

"She did." He began gathering the empty boxes and plastic totes. "She and my sister."

"Not you?"

"I inherited my dad's complete lack of artistic talent."

Kiera laughed softly only to catch herself. When had she last spontaneously reacted to something? *Someone?*

The answer was easy. Fifteen months ago. Before Joshua was murdered and her life imploded.

Sensing the marshal's stare, Kiera turned in her direction. Indeed, the other woman was scrutinizing her with the same laser focus she'd been aiming at Nash.

Kiera sat up straighter. She'd done nothing wrong and had no reason to feel guilty. So what if she'd laughed at Nash's joke? It meant nothing.

Another blast of strong wind rattled the windows. Though no later than mid-morning, it might as well have been twilight. Not a single sliver of sunlight penetrated the heavy clouds and dense snowfall. Kiera squinted, but other than the tops of pine trees, she couldn't see more than a few feet past the front porch.

"Wow," she commented a bit nervously. "It's nasty out there."

No sooner had she said it than a loud metallic bang sounded from the front porch. Then another. And a third, each growing in intensity.

The marshal exploded from the recliner. "What was that?"

Kiera sucked in a startled gasp and reached for Heather, unsure if she should shield her daughter with her body or grab her and run for their lives.

Nash started toward the window. "I'll take a look."

"Myers, stay put," the marshal ordered. "Kiera, get down. Now!"

Kiera didn't hesitate and threw herself onto the floor, scooping Heather beneath her. Every sound in the room increased in volume. The tick-tock of the clock. The hum of the furnace. The rapid beat of her heart. Kiera's skin grew tight, and her hands shook as panic signals spread through her system at lightning speed. From her vantage point on the floor, she watched Nash completely disregard the marshal's warning and inch toward the window.

The banging continued, the echo vibrating inside Kiera's head with the force of a hammer hitting wood. Suddenly, a shapeless shadow danced in front of the window, the scraping noise like a rake across metal.

She wanted to scream, but her voice refused to cooperate. What came out instead was a hoarse whisper. "Nash! Be careful!"

Marshal Gifford retreated several steps into the corner, reminding Kiera of a lioness stalking its prey. Her steely eyes never left the window. Or was it Nash they never left? When the shadow danced across the window again, she reached into her jacket. Withdrawing her Glock, she braced her legs and held the gun in front of her, using both hands to steady it.

"Move, Myers," she ordered.

He pivoted slowly and took her in, his gaze traveling from the gun to her face and back to the gun. "It's the wind," he said in an amazingly calm voice.

"I mean it, Myers. Get away from the window."

"No one's out there. The screen door must have come loose, and the wind is blowing it open and shut."

"I saw movement."

"The wind pushed one of the chairs across the porch." He held up his hands, palms facing forward. "I'm going to look outside and make sure. Don't shoot me."

The marshal stood motionless, her features chiseled from stone.

After a moment, Nash turned back around and eased toward the window. There, he tugged the curtain aside. The screen door—Kiera identified the sound now—banged and banged.

Tentatively, she began to rise.

"There's no one out there," Nash said with conviction, letting the curtain fall.

"Are you sure?" the marshal asked.

"I'll go outside and check."

"Not alone, you won't."

"You plan on shooting my porch chair?"

She didn't laugh. "I'm right behind you. Kiera, you stay down."

Then she and Nash were through the front door. From their voices and the scraping noises, Kiera determined Nash and the marshal were moving the chairs to their original positions. They weren't gone long. The marshal returned first and nodded at Kiera, who interpreted that as an all clear and climbed to her feet. Unbelievably, Heather had slept through the entire ordeal.

Nash fiddled with the screen door lock for several moments, testing it before closing it and the main door. Entering the living room, he assessed Kiera and the marshal, who'd re-holstered her gun and positioned herself next to the couch.

"So, it's Kiera," he said to her. "Not Tara."

She didn't answer.

He addressed the marshal. "I'm guessing Diane isn't your real name, either, and that you're not cousins on the way to your grandparents." When she didn't respond, he asked, "Which one of you is going to tell me who you really are and what's going on?"

The marshal replied before Kiera could. "Neither of us."

"You're staying in my home." He didn't wilt beneath the marshal's intimidating stare, for which Kiera gave him a lot of credit. "You might have died in that car, but I rescued you."

Marshal Gifford stood there a full twenty seconds before reaching slowly into her jacket again. Only this time, instead of her gun, she withdrew her badge.

"You're a US marshal." Nash had only a moment to glimpse the insignia before Diane—not her real name—returned the badge to her jacket pocket.

"Marshal Delana Gifford."

"Who's she?" He locked gazes with the woman he'd been calling Tara for the last day.

Her eyes asked for understanding and forgiveness.

"You don't need to know," Marshal Gifford snapped. "What's important is that we're on official business. And it's crucial we get back on the road as soon as possible. Also we need to contact the Marshals' office and advise them of our location. A lot of people are depending on us."

"What do *you* say?" He hadn't looked away from Kiera.

She swallowed and then straightened with that subtle fortitude of hers. "Kiera is my real name. Tara's the one I've been using this past year."

"Okay."

She'd been living under an alias. Who, he wondered, was she hiding from and why? Probably not an abusive husband. That wouldn't require her to be traveling in the company of a US marshal.

When neither woman spoke, Nash bent to pick up a stack of empty boxes. He had a lot of emotions to process and questions to ask. But, obviously, his guests weren't ready or willing to answer them. Better to wait until he and Kiera were alone. She'd be more likely to open up without the marshal nearby.

"Well, now that introductions are over," he said, sending the marshal an arched look, "I'm taking these upstairs. Will you be coming with me like usual or are we finally past that?"

"I'm heading outside to the shed. Reception may be better there." She turned to address Kiera. "Will you and Heather be okay?"

"Yes. I'll help Nash finish decorating."

"You don't have to." The marshal's dismissive tone implied since their cover had been blown, Kiera was no longer obligated to maintain pretenses.

Nash agreed. "She's right."

"I want to," Kiera insisted and knelt to check on Heather. With tender hands, she refastened a snap under the baby's chin that had come undone. "I can't stand being cooped up and need to stay busy."

Nash could relate. For him, however, it wasn't the confinement or boredom triggering his agitation. He'd had a lot thrown at him in the last day, especially the last few minutes. Mindless work would give him the opportunity to process everything and frame those questions he intended to ask Kiera later.

He lifted the boxes and started toward the stairs. In the bedroom, he stooped and entered the cubby, glad for a moment alone. He needed to put some distance between himself and Kiera, even just temporarily. Easier to put his feelings and the situation in perspective without an audience.

She was practically a stranger, he reminded himself. One with a mysterious past, a complicated life and in difficult circumstances, whatever those turned out to be. Not a friend or…more.

Before leaving the cubby, he rearranged the remaining items in an attempt to create more storage space for his next load. Maybe, when his parents arrived, he and his dad would sort through this stuff and toss any of the junk they were no longer using.

As Nash crossed the bedroom, he glanced at Kiera's belongings for any clues about her. He saw nothing out of the ordinary. Then again, what had he expected? To spot a revolver peeking out from her suitcase or a piece of bloodstained clothing?

If not a criminal, then who was she? A witness in a federal trial? Nash didn't know a whole lot about the US Marshals, but wasn't one of their duties transporting individuals in the witness protection program? That would explain Marshal Gifford's over-the-top protectiveness and Kiera's initial tentativeness toward him. It would also explain their cover stories.

Then again, so would Kiera being a federal informant. She could have been arrested and struck a deal: a reduced sentence in exchange for her testimony. He shouldn't assume that she was a good person just because he liked her. Nor should he assume her Christianity was real and not part of Tara's made up character.

Except his gut told him her faith was the one genuine thing Kiera had taken from her old life into her new one.

What if Heather was the key to all this? Come to think of it, was Kiera even Heather's mother? She might be a nanny assigned by the US Marshals' office, and Heather the child of a high profile criminal.

Trotting down the stairs, he thought back on his previous experience with law enforcement. In his job as a compliance inspector, he dealt mostly with the sheriff's office and, on rare occasions, the Flagstaff police. Two years ago, when drug smugglers were using a small ranch in the mountain foothills east of Camp Verde to land their planes, Nash had been recruited to assist the DEA with their stakeouts. His familiarity with the area had come in handy and was the reason his superiors had recommended him for the assignment.

At the time, he'd understood God's purpose for his participation in the DEA's operation. But what plans did He have for Nash now? Was Nash simply to provide aid for Kiera and Marshal Gifford until they were back on the road? Or did God have something more significant in store for Nash?

Entering the living room, he found Kiera sitting in the rocking chair, Heather cradled in her arms. Their pose, similar to last night and the epitome of innocence, triggered a pang in his heart. Curbing his feelings for her wouldn't be easy.

He wanted to believe Kiera wasn't a criminal and her troubles weren't her fault. But he also needed to be a realist.

"Heather woke up hungry," she explained. "I usually give her solid food for this feeding, but I'm running low and trying to ration what's left."

Seeing the profound love and devotion on Kiera's face when she gazed at Heather had him immediately discarding his previous notion. She was undeniably Heather's mother.

"There's food in the pantry," he suggested.

"Baby food? Heather's young. She can only eat certain things."

"Like what?"

"Well, scrambled eggs. Strained oatmeal and vegetables and fruits. Sometimes I mash bananas, but there aren't any."

Nash gave up resisting and enjoyed the way her loose curls bounced charmingly whenever she moved her head. Eventually, he dragged himself away and returned to the boxes. There, he dug out several of his mom's treasured knickknacks.

"There's oatmeal in the pantry," he said.

"It has to be baby oatmeal."

"What's the difference?"

"Baby oatmeal is processed for easier digestion. And it has no additives."

"Most of the food we have is organic," he said.

"Really?"

"Dad started Mom on an all organic and anti-inflammatory diet a while ago because of her MS."

"Has it helped her?"

"Some. It certainly hasn't hurt. I think what's made the biggest difference is Dad's involvement in Mom's care. She pushed him away for a long time, and it damaged their relationship."

"Why? Or is that too personal of a question?"

"Mom was afraid that if Dad knew how sick she was and how much pain she was in, he'd see her as a burden and leave. He almost did, too, but not for that reason. He didn't understand why she was pushing him away and thought she'd fallen out of love with him."

"I'm so glad they found their way back to one another."

Nash cleared his throat before his emotions got the best of him. "Me, too."

"I can't fathom what it must be like dealing with a chronic disease."

"You can't until you're in the middle of it. There's no instruction book."

"Not to defend your mom, but we all cope differently

with the challenges life deals us. And those we love are bound to be affected."

Was she referring to herself?

She gathered Heather and stood up. "Mind if I have a look in the pantry?"

"Sure. Want me to go with you?"

Here, perhaps, was his chance to ask Kiera those questions. Sitting in the living room, the marshal could walk in on them at any moment.

"Thanks. That'd be great." Her smile bloomed brighter than before.

He suffered a wave of guilt at not being fully honest with her, only to rationalize it away. He was involved and needed to know what was going on. His parents could arrive before Kiera, Heather and the marshal were gone. If their presence here might put his family in any kind of danger, he had to know why.

Abandoning the trio of nutcrackers on the side table, he joined Kiera and led her to the pantry. At the door, he reached in and turned on the light. Three walls of floor-to-ceiling shelves greeted them. And while Nash's parents kept a respectable supply of nonperishable food on hand, they didn't come close to filling the pantry. As a result, the bottom and topmost shelves sat empty.

"Don't tell me," Kiera said, peering over his shoulder. "The previous owners stored enough food in here to feed an army."

"So the story goes, according to local gossip."

Heather gurgled excitedly as if adding her opinion. The three of them were close enough that she was able to grab hold of Nash's ear from behind and tug.

He chuckled. "Hey, kiddo."

"Sorry," Kiera apologized and shifted Heather to her other hip. "She's getting quite curious. And she can yank pretty hard. I don't dare wear jewelry."

"I have pretty tough ears."

Kiera looked unconvinced. "Don't say you weren't warned."

Here they were, interacting like two regular people. Not a potential criminal traveling with a US marshal and a man who should keep his distance but couldn't seem to help himself.

Reaching for the shelves on their right, he removed a glass mason jar.

"This is some homemade applesauce Mom bought at the community sale in October. Locally made, locally canned. It's pretty good. Completely natural. No sugar added."

Kiera took the jar in her free hand and studied the label. "Sounds good."

"There's also home-canned peaches."

"Do you have a food processor?"

"A blender for Mom's smoothies. Will that work?" Nash retrieved a jar of the peaches.

Kiera nodded. "I can also cook up the oatmeal and puree that in the blender with a little formula. I have plenty of that. As long as we're not stuck her more than another day or two, we should be fine."

Nash retreated a step to give Kiera more room to peruse the pantry's contents. "Why don't you have a look around? See if there's anything else you can use."

She squeezed past him and began inspecting the shelves. "I'll try these." She chose a can of carrots and one of green beans. "Heather's used to store-bought baby food and may turn up her nose."

"We'll figure something out."

"Thank you, Nash."

They stood close, only a few inches apart. Neither moved nor looked away.

Warning bells went off in Nash's head. Whatever was occurring between them wasn't a good idea for a multitude of reasons. He should put an end to it now before something happened. A touch. A word. A special smile. A kiss.

The next second, they were interrupted when the kitchen door opened and then banged closed.

"Marshal Gifford," Kiera whispered.

"Right."

"She must not have gotten any reception on her phone."

"And isn't happy about it."

The marshal stomped past them, unaware Nash and Kiera were in the pantry. Shortly after that, they heard her marching up the stairs.

Kiera didn't call out to the marshal. Nash tried not to read any significance into that. Her not drawing attention to them may have nothing to do with Nash or any interest Kiera might have in him.

"Tell me," he said in a low voice. "Are you safe with the marshal?"

"Absolutely."

"She's highly reactive."

"Because of her training. That's what makes her good at her job."

"But you are in danger from someone?"

Kiera nodded and, it seemed instinctively, drew Heather closer to her.

Nash decided to tell her what he'd overheard, believing she should know. "Did the marshal mention she got through to someone on her phone?"

"No!" Kiera drew back. "When? Who?"

"Earlier this morning. She was in the upstairs bathroom leaving a message while I was getting the nativity scene out of the cubby. Whoever she called, I think she was warning them."

"Of what?" Surprise and concern flashed in Kiera's wide eyes.

"I don't know. She told the person to be careful and to trust no one. She ended by saying she loved them."

"So, it was a family member or friend she called?"

"That would be my guess."

Kiera shifted a fraction nearer to Nash so that Heather was cocooned between them. "I'm…confused. Why didn't she tell me?"

"Watch yourself around her, Kiera." He resisted the urge to put a protective arm around her.

"I will. But are you sure you're not overreacting?"

"If she hid the call from you, rest assured she's hiding something else."

"There has to be an explanation. She probably just hasn't had a chance to tell me."

He heard the doubt creeping into her voice. "Kiera. I want to help you. But I need you to tell me what's going on. Who are you running from and why?"

She swallowed. "I wish I could tell you. I really do. But it's too risky. I'd never forgive myself if something happened to you."

Her sincerity rang true, and he began to believe she returned his growing fondness for her.

"Maybe one day?"

"Maybe." Her demeanor softened. "I'd like that."

"Is there a possibility we'll see each other again?"

"No, I... I'm not sure why I said what I did." She sighed. "Never mind."

Nash refused to let the moment pass. Whatever this was felt real and worth pursuing. "Here's an idea. I give you my number. If you decide you want to hear from me again, call me."

Her shoulders slumped. "My life is complicated right now. I'm not sure when it will ever be uncomplicated. I won't make promises I can't keep. That wouldn't be fair."

"Okay." He hid his disappointment by reaching for the box of oatmeal.

She was right, and the fact was, he shouldn't involve himself with someone obviously in trouble. He'd be asking for hurt and disappointment. She probably didn't live in Kingman, or have family in Flagstaff, for that matter. Long distance relationships were hard enough without adding in complexities and secrets.

The atmosphere between them had changed. Kiera abruptly left the pantry. Nash followed, carrying the jars. Heather began to fuss and Kiera patted her back as she returned her to the baby seat and fastened her in.

"I'll get the blender." Nash opened a lower cabinet, retrieved the small appliance and straightened.

Kiera came up beside him and said in a low voice, "I wish things were different."

"Me, too." He set the blender down and faced her. "If God sees fit for our paths to cross again, then they will."

"Yes. We'll leave it in His hands." She reached for a jar—and froze at what sounded like someone climbing the front porch steps. "What's that? Is someone here?"

"Could be the wind again. I'll take a look."

"Okay," Kiera agreed, a quiver in her voice.

Before he could assure her there was nothing to worry about, three loud raps echoed through the cabin. She jumped, shrieked and grabbed his arm.

"Hello," a muffled shout came through the front door. "Anyone home?"

"Who's that?" Kiera began to tremble.

The marshal's footsteps sounded through the cabin as she ran down the stairs.

Nash didn't hesitate. "Get Heather," he told Kiera, "and the two of you stay out of sight. Don't come into the living room for any reason until I give you the all clear. And try not to panic. It's probably a county worker alerting residents about road conditions or the Sheriff's Department verifying we're all right."

"Be careful, Nash. Please."

"I'll be right back."

As he strode toward the front door, he prayed whoever stood on the other side was a casual visitor and not the person after Kiera.

Chapter Five

Marshal Gifford was standing at the front door when Nash got there. Her scowl transmitted in precise detail exactly how she felt about their unexpected visitor.

"Where's Kiera and Heather?" she demanded.

"Safe. In the kitchen. I told her to stay out of sight."

"Don't answer the door."

"Whoever it is could have important information about the blizzard. Or need help."

"They could also intend to blow our heads off."

"They've already seen me." Nash hitched his chin at the tall panel of textured glass beside the door.

"Okay. You can open the door." The marshal positioned herself out of sight, her hand hovering near her concealed weapon. "Only a crack. Don't let them inside under any circumstances regardless of what they say. And be ready for any fast moves."

"Is that necessary?" He pointed to her side where the Glock hid beneath her jacket.

Her scowl deepened.

"I highly doubt whoever's after you and Kiera traveled through this blizzard and found you here."

Three more loud raps sounded, causing both of them to startle reflexively.

"Quit arguing with me, Myers," the marshal snapped, "and send the person away."

Kiera may trust this woman, but not Nash. Something about her didn't sit right with him. He'd felt that way even before she'd lied to him about her phone getting service. He conceded his reaction to her might be due to her abrasive manner. Only that didn't explain her lying to him.

Nash peered through the glass and saw a bundled-up figure bent at the waist, removing a snowshoe. "It's a man. I can't tell if he's in uniform or not." He opened the door a few inches, letting in a blast of frigid air. "Hello."

Their visitor popped upright and, with a gloved hand, pulled down the scarf covering his mouth and nose. "Well, good day."

Behind him, falling snow formed a dense white curtain. Nash was impressed the man had walked through the blizzard from wherever he came.

"I'm your neighbor. Lester Ahrens." He removed his protective goggles. "I bought the Wheeler place a few months ago." He plucked off his right glove and extended his hand.

"Right." Nash opened the door wider, a blast of cold air hitting him. He accepted the offered handshake, trying to recall what he'd been told about Lester. "My folks mentioned meeting you at Hillside Community Church."

"Oh, yeah. That's right." He beamed. "They're great.

Really nice people. Everyone in Wild Wind Hills is. Your parents especially have gone out of their way to make me feel welcome. Are they around by chance?" He craned his neck in an effort to peer inside.

"No. They're stuck in Flagstaff and waiting for a break in the weather."

Lester's features fell. "That's a shame. I was looking forward to seeing them again. How you doing, by the way? Some storm, huh? Glad it's finally letting up." His cheeks had begun to redden from the cold, and he stomped his feet in an attempt to keep warm. "You need anything? I have plenty of food and supplies and firewood at my place if you're running low."

"We're good. Thanks, though. Kind of you to offer."

"We?" Lester craned his neck again.

"Some friends are with me."

"Cool." He glanced sideways over his shoulder. "I just came from Mrs. Smithson's. You worry about someone her age, you know."

"You do," Nash agreed and opened the door farther as his suspicions abated.

"She put me to work. I cleared the snow from her back stoop and carried out her trash to the dumpster behind her house. Afraid her little dog didn't like me much."

"He's very protective. Doesn't like anyone. Last time I was there, he almost bit my finger off when I tried to pet him."

Nash shot the marshal a sideways glance that said, "This guy's for real." How could he know about Nash's parents, Mrs. Smithson and her little Pomeranian if he wasn't who he claimed to be?

Her responding glance said she was less convinced.

"Hey," Lester said. "Any chance I can trouble you for a coffee before I head back? Mrs. Smithson's an herbal tea drinker and didn't have any."

The old woman did like her teas. His remark further convinced Nash that his family's new neighbor was no danger to them. He sent the marshal a second glance. She shook her head vigorously.

"I promise not to take up too much of your time." Lester crossed his arms over his chest and rubbed his upper arms. Clearly, he was cold.

"It's not that."

He retreated and dropped his arms, his features reflecting his disappointment. "Sorry. Not my intention to intrude. I'm sure you're busy with your friends."

Guilt ate at Nash. His parents would be ashamed of him for turning Lester away. They prided themselves on their hospitality. And Lester had said nothing suspicious. He was who he claimed to be: the new owner of the Wheeler place.

Nash almost invited Lester inside. Almost. He hesitated, recalling Kiera's face when she'd heard Lester at the door. She'd been terrified, and he couldn't bring himself to cause her more fear. Then, there was the marshal's warning to consider. He may not fully trust the woman, but Kiera did. And for her sake, he'd defer to the marshal. This time.

"Hey, man," he said to Lester. "I'm the one who's sorry." He shrugged. "But my friends, they're kind of indisposed at the moment. Stomach flu."

"Gotcha." Lester sighed and started to put on his glove.

Guilt ate at Nash. "How 'bout a cup of coffee for the road? I could meet you in the carport. That way, we won't disturb my friends." And the guy could escape the cold and wind for a few minutes.

"Sounds good. Thanks." Lester stooped to grab his snowshoes and, with a friendly wave over his shoulder, trotted down the steps.

Nash shut the door.

His long exhale was cut short when Marshal Gifford stuck a finger in his face. "The carport? Are you serious?"

"Ten minutes, and he'll be on his way."

"I'm taking Kiera and the baby upstairs. I repeat, under no circumstances, let that guy in the cabin. I'm locking all the doors behind you and will have my gun drawn."

"Understood."

Nash mock saluted and made his way toward the kitchen, telling himself nothing would go wrong.

He quickly threw on a jacket and cap and met Lester in the carport, a steaming mug in his hand.

"Thanks, man." Lester accepted the coffee, tested the temperature and then sipped gratefully. "That hits the spot. Mighty cold out there."

Sheltered from the snow and constant wind, Lester had removed his gloves and goggles, stuffing both in his pockets. His snug parka revealed wide shoulders and a trim physique.

"Glad to hear it," Nash said.

He'd taken considerable flack from the marshal over letting Lester into the carport. No sooner had she hustled Kiera and the baby upstairs than she'd immediately returned to stand guard on the other side of the mudroom door. Nash imagined her with her ear pressed close, listening intently.

"This blizzard came out of nowhere, didn't it?" Lester propped an elbow on the hood of Nash's truck, his stance casual and engaging. "I'd planned on heading home before Christmas. Guess that's not happening."

"I heard the snow's supposed to let up by this evening."

"Maybe the county will plow the roads tomorrow."

"Let's hope." Nash took the opportunity to change the subject. "What prompted you to buy a home in Wild Wind Hills? Mom says you're retiring soon and will be living here full-time."

"Indeed I will. Nothing like the country. Peace and quiet. Friendly people. Clean, fresh air." He inhaled robustly as if to emphasize his point.

He looked too young to retire, Nash thought. Fifty at most. Then again, he could be an avid fitness enthusiast or one of those people blessed with a youthful appearance. He definitely had the physique of a younger man.

He may also be very successful financially and able to retire early. The Wheeler place hadn't sold for cheap. Nash recalled his parents talking about it.

"What is it you do again?" he asked.

"I'm in corporate sales. And, believe me, I'm sick of the rat race and ready to leave it behind. Trading a desk chair for a recliner is my goal in life."

"When will that be?"

"Next summer, if all goes well and the stock market cooperates."

"If you don't mind me saying, you look young to retire."

Lester grinned broadly. "I invested my retirement fund wisely these past few years. Made a bundle. I can give you the name of my broker if you're interested—" He went silent and tilted his ear in the direction of the door. "Is that one of your friends?"

"Must be." Nash acted as if he hadn't heard the scuffling sound.

"I'd sure like to meet them."

"They're really not feeling well. Tomorrow or the day after might be better. My parents should be here by then." Nash attempted to distract his visitor. "How's your internet, by the way? You have service? Our dish is out. The wind did a number on it."

"I've been using a mobile hot spot, but that hasn't worked since yesterday. I need to get a dish like you."

He and Lester discussed various satellite providers for several minutes. Nash was about to make an excuse to Lester when the other man saved him the trouble.

"I should probably hit the road." He drained the last of his coffee and chuckled. "If I can find it."

Nash took the mug and walked with Lester to the carport opening. There, Lester put on his gloves and goggles and stepped into his snowshoes.

"Thanks for stopping by," Nash said. "It was nice meeting you."

"Same here, Nash. I'll be seeing you soon." Lester straightened after buckling his snowshoes. "Maybe tomorrow."

"Yeah." Tomorrow, if the roads were plowed and his houseguests had left. "Have a Merry Christmas."

Nash watched Lester trudge across the snow and down the driveway. When he was out of sight, Nash returned to the mudroom door and found it locked.

He knocked briskly and called to the marshal waiting on the other side. "It's me, Marshal Gifford. Lester's gone."

He heard the lock disengage and, a moment later, the door opened a few inches. She peered past him.

"I'm alone." Nash stepped aside to let her see. "I promise."

She wavered, indecision on her face.

Kiera suddenly materialized behind her. "The guy left. I saw him through the upstairs window."

Only then did the marshal allow Nash into the cabin. She slammed the door shut behind him and locked it. "That was foolish of you, talking to him," she groused as all three of them returned to the kitchen. "And very risky."

"The guy was freezing and wanted a cup of coffee. I wasn't about to tell him no. And since he didn't pull a gun on me, I'm pretty sure he's harmless."

"How do you know? You haven't met him before."

"Don't be so hard on Nash," Kiera admonished. Heather lay against her shoulder, sleeping soundly, her thumb in her mouth. "Nash was just being nice. And like he said, nothing bad happened. If the man was sent by—" She stopped short. "We wouldn't be standing here, arguing."

"Nothing bad happened *this* time."

"Just tell me what's going on?" Nash demanded, weary of getting the runaround. "Who's after you, and why are you so afraid?"

"We can't involve you." The marshal turned and walked away.

"Can't? Or won't?"

She spun on him. "You're safer not knowing. And we're safer, too."

"No one will find you here. Not unless they can somehow track you."

Kiera blanched. "Is that possible?"

"No," the marshal insisted. "It's not."

"Are you positive?"

The marshal's demeanor unexpectedly gentled, and she put a hand on Kiera's shoulder. "Don't worry. I'm sure Myers is right. That guy was who he claimed to be. I overreacted. No need to panic."

Kiera nodded, though her cheeks remained pale.

What had instilled such fear in her and such protectiveness in the marshal? Nash's thoughts were interrupted by his phone playing a George Strait song.

"It's my mom." He withdrew his phone from his pocket.

Kiera stared at him in shock. "You have service?"

"It can happen. A shift in the clouds."

He sent the marshal a look, reminding her about this morning and overhearing her on her phone. She refused to be intimidated and squared her shoulders.

"Thank God." Kiera snuggled Heather closer, hope shining in her eyes.

He dug his phone out of his shirt pocket and put it to his ear. "Hello, Mom?"

"Oh, sweetheart." She bit back a sob. "I'm so glad I got through. We've been trying nonstop since yesterday. Are you all right? The weather reports have me and your dad worried sick. I'm glad you made it to the cabin before the blizzard hit."

Her panicked voice reached him through the static and triggered a rush of love and relief. He'd been worried about them, too. "I'm fine, Mom. How are you?" The cold sometimes aggravated her MS and caused her considerable pain.

"I'm fine. No worse than usual. The hotel bed's pretty comfortable."

In the background, Nash heard his dad saying something about the weather forecast and them driving up tomorrow or the day after. His mom tried her best to relay the information, but his dad kept talking over her.

"Can his parents get a message through for us?" Kiera asked the marshal.

"Possibly. Let me think." She had her phone out and was checking for service. For whatever reason, she wasn't getting any. "Kiera, check your phone, too."

"Can you repeat that, Mom?" Nash turned away from her and Kiera, unable to follow two separate conversations.

"Lester Ahrens called your dad," his mom said. "Asked us to run by his house. He's worried about the roof caving in from the weight of the snow. I told him we were stuck in Flagstaff."

"Really? Because he was just here."

"Are you sure? He told us he was planning on driving up this week but had an accident. He slipped in the shower and had to get six stitches right above his eye. Can you believe it? Poor guy."

"What?" There'd been no stitches anywhere on Lester's face. No bandage. No evidence of an injury.

"It was a little scary," his mom continued. "He lives alone and wound up driving himself to the emergency room."

Nash struggled to process this latest development. If Lester was still in Phoenix, who was the man he'd given coffee to? And why the pretense? What, if anything, did he have to do with Kiera and the marshal?

"Mom. Are you a hundred percent positive? Mom? Mom?"

She didn't answer. The next second, his phone beeped, and when he examined the screen, it read no service. The same thing had happened earlier with the marshal, service lasting only a minute or two.

He ground his teeth together in frustration and stuffed his phone back in his pocket. "I lost her."

"What was that you were saying about your neighbor?" the marshal asked, an edge to her voice.

Nash started to respond, only to clamp his mouth shut. His mom could have been mistaken. MS, and some of her medications, affected her memory and caused occasional confusion. She'd been wrong before about people, places and events. Maybe someone else had fallen in the shower. Or Lester's injury was on the side of his head, rather than near his eye, and hidden by the cap he'd worn.

Plus, Nash and his mom hadn't had the best connection. The marshal and Kiera had also been talking in background, as well as his dad. The fact was Nash might have misheard his mom.

Then there was his distrust of the marshal. She'd lied to him and probably to Kiera. Nash liked Kiera, but the fact was, she could be a criminal, and the one he should be careful around, not the marshal.

Until he knew one way or the other about Lester, or Kiera and the marshal finally leveled with him, he'd keep this information to himself.

"Just that he'd called them," he answered the marshal's question with a nonchalance he didn't feel.

If only he could access the internet and conduct a few searches, he might learn something. Possibly find a picture of Lester on social media or his company's website. Locate a news article about a young woman and her baby.

"Kiera, you going to be okay if I go outside and try my phone again?" The marshal pulled up the collar of her shirt and fastened the top button.

"Yeah. Of course." Kiera shifted Heather to her other side and began sorting through the food items she and Nash had brought from the pantry.

He set the coffee mug in the sink. The man who'd just left the cabin *had* to be Lester. Nothing else made sense. How else would he have known about Mrs. Smithson and her little dog and love of tea?

Except, what if his mom was right and the real Lester Ahrens was in Phoenix?

"Wait," Nash called after the marshal. "I'll go with you. I want to try my phone again, too."

Chapter Six

Kiera sat at the kitchen table with Heather, who was once again propped up in her baby seat. Kiera didn't miss Fresno or her job or her condo. She'd never formed an attachment to any of them. But she missed the convenience of her daughter's high chair at home. Also her crib and changing table.

And she missed Fort Worth and her old job as a data architect. Strange, really, considering she was from Connecticut. She'd moved after receiving a job offer with a tech firm and fallen in love with Fort Worth's colorful Western history and hospitable people. Not long after, she'd met Joshua, and it felt like her life had finally come together.

Somehow, his betrayal hadn't affected her homesickness for Fort Worth and her former job. Knowing she could never return to Fort Worth, never see her family again left a large empty hole in her heart nothing other than her daughter filled.

Kiera reached out and stroked her daughter's cheek.

"I wish you could meet your grandma and grandpa."
The rest of her family, too.

Heather gurgled.

"That's what I say. Someday."

She prayed the 7-Crowns Syndicate would lose interest in her after a few years, but if their number two—Edward Lyons, aka The Chairman—was found guilty because of her testimony, the likelihood remained she, and possibly Heather, would be living under assumed identities for the rest of her lives.

The thought of telling her sweet little girl about the criminal activities that had led to her father's murder filled Keira with dread. She'd give anything to have her family by her side when the day came.

Pushing aside her misery before it overwhelmed her, Kiera returned her attention to the diaper bag. While the marshal and Nash were outside checking the service on their phones, she'd been busy. First, she'd organized several meals for Heather from the food she and Nash had found in the pantry. There was more than enough for two days. Possibly longer. Now she was inventorying her remaining baby supplies.

Surely, the US Marshals' office was searching for them and had alerted local law enforcement to be on the lookout. They'd be located before long, especially once the marshal's disabled car was spotted. Kiera had to believe the trial wouldn't proceed without her. At the least, her testimony would be postponed until her arrival.

"Please, Lord," she whispered. "Let it stop snowing." The sooner she could testify, the sooner she could return to Fresno and feel safe again, or as safe as anyone in her position could feel.

While Heather wiggled her feet and gnawed on a teething ring, Kiera picked through the diaper bag. She still had plenty of powdered formula. Disposable diapers? Not so many.

That didn't worry her as much as running low on food had. She'd found a stack of old dish towels in the kitchen drawer. If push came to shove, she'd ask Nash about using them for makeshift diapers. Not a perfect solution, but doable. Of course, she'd reimburse him for any cost.

What she really wanted was for him or the marshal to reach someone on their phones. Granted, the weather was probably enough to keep the syndicate at bay, but it was also preventing help from getting to them.

"After this, we'll finish with the decorations," she told Heather. "You can help me hang tinsel on the tree."

At Heather's silly smile, Kiera's mood improved. Her life could be worse. Much worse. She had her daughter, which was far better than being alone.

A moment later, she heard the door in the mudroom open and shuffling footsteps. Then Nash came in, the marshal right behind him. Their cheeks were flushed from the cold and their hair tousled from their caps. The disarray gave Nash an appealingly boyish look.

"Any success?" Kiera asked, but she already knew the answer from their glum expressions.

"None," the marshal said. "But the snow isn't as bad as it was."

"Well, that's good news." Kiera looked to Nash for confirmation. Except he'd gone to the refrigerator for a bottled water and had his back to her.

"I'll be upstairs." The marshal tromped off without waiting for a response.

Kiera shrugged. The marshal wasn't mad at her, just mad at events.

Nash, too. He downed the bottled water in several long gulps, then crumpled the bottle with unnecessary force and tossed it in the recycle bin beneath the sink.

Maybe he was still bothered by the marshal not being truthful about her phone call in the bathroom earlier.

Heather's sudden whimper distracted Kiera.

"What's wrong, little one?" she asked.

Nash came over to the table and retrieved the teething ring from the floor. "She dropped this."

"Thanks." She got up and washed the teething ring in the sink, then sat back down.

Nash slid into the chair beside her. "Marshal Gifford is right. The snow isn't as bad."

"What does that mean as far as her and I being able to leave?"

Kiera gave the teething ring to Heather. But by now, the baby had lost interest and was staring at Nash. Not that Kiera blamed her daughter. She'd stared at Nash a few times herself today.

"I'm not sure," he said, playfully tweaking Heather's chin. The baby beamed at him as if he were made of sunshine and lollipops. "Other than I'm more inclined to go out on the snowmobile. Leave you and the marshal here."

"She won't like that. She'll want to go with you."

"She won't have a choice. And, besides, she's the one with a gun. You're not out of danger yet, are you?"

He wanted her to level with him. Kiera could hear the question even if he hadn't voiced it.

She sighed. "I'm probably going to need protection to some degree for the rest of my life."

"Is it really that bad?"

Tears pricked her eyes, not the reaction she'd expected of herself. She'd believed she was stronger after all this time. She'd been through so much.

"I don't know how I got here. How my life took such a wrong turn. I go back in my mind all the time, trying to find the warning signs I missed. I've prayed until I'm empty inside, and I still don't have an answer other than God is sending me along the path He needs me to be on." She sniffed and wiped at her damp cheeks. "Where the marshal and I are going, what I'll be doing when I get there, it's possible I can save lives. If nothing else, justice will be served. That's important to me."

"You're not a criminal, then?"

"No! What gave you that idea? Wait. Don't bother. I can see how you'd draw that conclusion."

Something happened then, something Kiera hadn't anticipated and hadn't realized how very much she craved: Nash took her hand in his. He folded her fingers inside his larger stronger ones as naturally and purposefully as if they belonged there.

All other thoughts deserted her as she reveled in the warmth and comfort of his touch. Too much time had passed since she'd last experienced human contact that wasn't casual or perfunctory or accidental.

"I can't imagine what you've been through," he said softly. "But I can see the impact of it, the constant fear in your eyes and the scars on your soul." He gave her hand a gentle squeeze. "I also see how brave you are. Whatever ordeal you're facing, it's not small and not easy. I admire you for pushing forward despite the risks. That requires a lot of faith. In God. In yourself. In your purpose."

How did he see what others missed?

"Kiera, I refuse to accept that me finding you is random. God has a reason."

"Nash." The tears threatened to return. "I…just… I can't make any promises right now. Not until…"

"I understand."

She doubted that. She barely understood herself sometimes.

With tremendous reluctance, she withdrew her hand, wishing things were different. If only she'd met Nash a year from now while pushing Heather in a stroller down her street or at her church during fellowship hour after Sunday service. Then, maybe, possibly, they'd have a teeny-tiny chance. He did like Heather, and being good with children was paramount to Kiera.

He'd also have to be incredibly accepting and willing to make sacrifices. Kiera wouldn't lie about her past. But any man she met and fell in love with, and who shared her life, needed to keep her secrets at all costs. There was always the chance that, if the 7-Crowns Syndicate found her, she and Heather would have to relocate all over again. Nash didn't strike her as the kind to willingly leave his family behind, perhaps forever. More than loving his parents and sister, he played a vital role in his mom's care. He'd also be an uncle soon.

He couldn't simply walk away, regardless of how

much he might love someone. And she couldn't ask him, or anyone.

Kiera had to accept her circumstances for what they were. She'd be on her own for the rest of her life. Imagining herself with Nash, with anyone, was inviting heartache.

In an effort to rein in her emotions, she asked, "If I run out of diapers for Heather, can I use some of the old dish towels in the drawer over there? I'll pay you for them."

Nash smiled, sadly and, yet, with amusement. "You can have the dish towels. There's no need to pay me."

"I think I have some diaper pins in here."

She shifted the diaper bag on her lap. Opening a side compartment, she rummaged through the contents, encountering rash cream, a pacifier, a random bottle cap, a pen and a single sock. But no pins.

When she moved to the third compartment, Nash asked, "Need any help?"

"I appreciate that, but I know what I'm looking for."

Naturally, she found the pins in the last place left to look—at the bottom of a small zippered pocket on the inside of the diaper bag. As she pulled out the pins, her fingertips encountered something unfamiliar.

"What in the world?" She extracted a small squarish black object about the size of a key fob. "I didn't put this in here. Kind of looks like the personal alarm my grandma carries. Except I don't have one."

"Can I see it?"

She passed him the object, concern growing. "Do you know what it is? Must have been in there a while."

He turned the object over in his hand. "Who's had access to your diaper bag?"

"No one."

"What about the marshal?"

Kiera shook her head. "The bag's been with me the entire time." Her pulse started to beat triple time. "Why? What is it?"

"I could be wrong, I'm no expert, but I think it's a tracking device."

"I thought the marshal said that was impossible."

His serious tone intensified, as did his gaze on her. "Someone's keeping tabs on your location."

"Dear Lord." Kiera pressed her hands to her mouth as an icy spear of alarm sliced through her. It was happening. What she'd feared the most. "Can they find me? Will the blizzard interfere with the signal?"

"I'm not familiar enough with tracking devices to say."

"What am I going to do?" Her voice rose, then broke. "What am I going to do?" she repeated.

"Who's after you, Kiera?"

"Bad people. I'm in trouble. Real trouble. Where's Marshal Gifford?" She sprang to her feet and grabbed Heather, wrestling her daughter free from the baby seat. Running toward the stairs, she hollered, "Marshal Gifford! They found me."

Heather began to cry.

Kiera felt Nash behind her and spun. He still held the tracker.

"What's wrong?" The marshal ran down the stairs like a soldier charging into battle.

"Someone planted a tracker on me. Nash, show her." Kiera's words tumbled out. "I found it in the diaper bag."

The marshal thrust out her hand. "Give it to me."

Nash passed her the device. Kiera noticed him studying the marshal, a wary expression on his face. Did he suspect her of playing some part in this? No. She was Kiera and Heather's protector.

"Is it a tracker?" Kiera was simultaneously desperate to know and afraid of the answer.

The marshal's response was to drop the device on the floor and crush it beneath the heel of her boot. "We're not safe here."

Nash sat on the couch, watching Kiera pace nervously with Heather in her arms. Marshal Gifford stood guard near the window—her usual position where she could see out but not be seen. No amount of willpower stopped his right knee from bouncing.

"Who's after you and why?" he asked.

Kiera drew up short and stared at him as if she hadn't understood. All color had drained from her face, and she pushed at her tousled hair. "We have to leave. You said yourself the snow isn't falling as hard as before."

"We can't leave," he said. "Not in my truck. The roads aren't clear. We won't get a hundred yards before we're trapped in a pile of snow."

The marshal didn't counter him, which he found interesting. She was always the first to insist they leave. What about finding the tracker accounted for the change in her?

Kiera resumed her pacing. "If we stay here, they'll find me."

Nash stood. "Our odds are better holding off an intruder from inside the cabin than escaping one on foot. Don't you agree, Marshal?"

She continued staring out the window. "Yes."

"Who did you call earlier?"

No answer.

"I heard you leaving a message."

"Did you get through to the Marshals' office?" Kiera rushed forward, Heather bouncing in her arms. "Are they sending someone for us? Why didn't you tell me?"

The marshal's eyes narrowed. "I wasn't able to reach them."

"Then who exactly did you call?" Nash asked.

Again, no answer.

"Tell us," Kiera insisted.

She turned from the window at last. "It's not what you think."

"What I think is you're hiding something."

Marshal Gifford swallowed. Paused. Finally, she said, "I called my son."

Nash hadn't expected that, or her answer to strike him as the honest truth. If he had only one phone call to make in what might be a life or death situation, it would be to a family member.

"Will he contact the Marshals' office?" Kiera asked weakly, as if she already knew the answer was no.

"I only had a few seconds before I lost service."

And she'd used those seconds to warn her son to be careful. Of what? Nash thought her reaction to seeing the tracker had been anger rather than surprise or fear. Did she know more than she was telling? Like who might have planted it?

"You have a son." Kiera placed a kiss on the top of Heather's head. "You must want to get back to him."

"Yes. I do."

She returned to the window, demonstrating in no uncertain terms the discussion of her personal life was at an end.

"How soon until they find us?" Kiera resumed her previous pacing.

"I haven't a clue. There's no way of telling how long the tracker was in your bag or if it was even active and sending a signal."

Nash considered for a moment before saying, "They, whoever they are, might already be here."

Her eyes widened. "In Wild Wind Hills?"

"Next door, but I can't be certain."

That got the marshal's attention. She abandoned her post at the window. "Tell me everything."

Kiera stumbled toward the rocking chair and collapsed into it, folding her body protectively over Heather's. "Oh, please, God. Don't let them hurt my baby. She's all I have."

The agony in her voice tore at Nash. Suddenly, he wanted to do everything in his power to help her and her daughter.

He squared off against the marshal. "I'll tell you on one condition. You fill me in on what's happening. No more excuses about it being too dangerous. I think we're long past that, don't you?"

"This isn't a game, Myers."

"Tell him, tell him," Kiera cried, rocking Heather with her entire body. "We don't have much time."

He braced himself for the marshal's outburst. Instead, she nodded briskly. "All right. Fine. Kiera's in WITSEC."

"What's that?"

"Witness protection. She saw…someone murdered last year by a very powerful criminal with connections to organized crime. Her testimony could put him away for life."

"My husband was killed by Edward Lyons," Kiera blurted. "The 7-Crowns Syndicate's number two. Right in our backyard. And now they're trying to eliminate me so I can't testify."

Nash retreated a step, stunned by the news. His glance cut between the two women. Kiera's lower lip trembled. The marshal looked ready to run through a brick wall if necessary to protect Kiera. This was no fabricated story. They were serious. Deadly serious.

"We picked up Kiera yesterday morning," the marshal continued. "But outside Kingman, my partner suffered a pulmonary embolism and had to be hospitalized. Kiera and I were supposed to rendezvous with another marshal in Flagstaff, but the blizzard hit and we went off the road."

Nash inhaled deeply. Once. Twice. He needed a minute for everything to sink in.

Kiera couldn't seem to sit still and pushed out of the rocking chair. "What's going to happen?"

"Wait," Nash said, confused. "If they want to eliminate you, why didn't they do it when they were close enough to plant the tracker? Why let you lead them on a chase halfway across the country? It makes no sense."

His observation must have stumped both Kiera and the marshal for they looked bewildered.

"Maybe it wasn't the right time or place," the marshal finally offered. "Too risky. They're probably waiting for the right opportunity."

"Seems like they weren't worried about time or place when they killed Kiera's husband in their backyard and with her watching. Why now?"

The marshal glared at him. "You know zip about this organization or what they're capable of. They could be taking extra precautions because they're being watched closely."

Nash rubbed his temples. He felt off-kilter, his world abruptly altered like he'd stepped through Alice's looking glass. He couldn't believe he was having a conversation about murder and a crime syndicate and Kiera being targeted for elimination. It was a wonder she could even function after all she'd been through.

"The diaper bag hasn't been out of my condo for days," Kiera said, her fear and frustration visibly rising. "I haven't been out for days."

"They're professionals," the marshal said. "They could have broken into your house without you noticing."

Kiera's features crumpled, and she bit back a scared sob.

"I still don't buy it," Nash said, convinced the marshal was being intentionally obtuse or lying. "This 7-Crowns Syndicate is apparently stealthy enough to break into Kiera's home and plant a tracker but didn't bother to eliminate her then? No. Something's not right."

"Your turn, Myers," she snapped. "What makes you think 7-Crowns has found us?"

"*Maybe* found you."

"I'm listening."

He perched on the arm of the couch. The marshal wouldn't like what he had to say.

"The man who showed up here earlier, Lester Ahrens, there's a chance he's not who he claimed to be."

"And you're just telling us now!"

"What makes you doubt he's your neighbor?" Kiera asked, her voice strained.

"He's new here, and I've never met him. But my parents have. Mom told me when she called that Lester was home in Phoenix. Not in Wild Wind Hills. According to her, he recently fell in the shower and banged his forehead bad enough to require stitches. The man here today didn't have a bandage or stitches or any indication of a wound."

Kiera released a low moan of despair. The marshal muttered under her breath.

"My mom could be wrong," Nash hastened to add. "She has MS. That and her meds can affect her memory. She's not always reliable. And our phone connection was terrible. I had trouble hearing her over the static."

"We're not taking any chances," the marshal said. "We're going to assume your mom was right."

"But again, if the man here today was from the 7-Crowns Syndicate, why didn't he pull a gun on me? He'd know Kiera was here from the tracker."

The marshal growled angrily. "I don't have all the answers. But I do have questions. What can we do to protect ourselves? You said there are no guns in the cabin."

"No." Nash shoved off the couch arm, suddenly energized. "There are other things we can use for weapons."

"Like?"

"Shovels. Hammers. A baseball bat. A pocket knife. Kitchen knives." He reached for the tool set sitting beside the fireplace and removed the poker from the rack. "This."

Kiera's eyes widened.

"That's not much," the marshal scoffed.

"There's also some wooden planks in the shed from when my dad repaired the steps to the bunker. I can use them to barricade the front and back doors."

"What about the windows?"

"I'll figure out a way to barricade them, too."

She studied Nash before giving him a curt nod. "Let's gather every potential weapon and then meet up in the kitchen. Did I see a fire extinguisher in the pantry? Grab that, too. I'll start in the carport." With that, she walked out.

Nash went over to Kiera and placed a hand on her shoulder. "Are you going to be all right?"

"Do you really believe that man wasn't your neighbor?"

"I pray he was and my mom's wrong."

"Me, too."

"But even if he is Lester, there's still the tracker."

Tears gathered in her eyes. He wanted to draw her into his embrace and promise to keep her safe.

Instead, he said, "You take care of Heather. I'll be back in a little while."

As much as he wanted to protect Kiera, he was no match for a professional hit man. Neither was the marshal, despite her training. Especially if there was more than one. He hadn't voiced his gravest concern: that the man pretending to be Lester might be one of several sent by 7-Crowns—all of them fully armed with weapons that would make her Glock look like a pea shooter. If that was the case, they were in serious trouble.

Thirty minutes later, they gathered in the kitchen. Laid out the table, or leaning against it, were the make-shift weapons Nash and the marshal had assembled. He thought again of professional hit men and how their paltry collection would be no match. Even so, they weren't completely defenseless. And thanks to finding the tracker, they wouldn't be caught off guard.

"Take your pick, Kiera," the marshal said, grabbing the axe and examining the blade. "What are you comfortable with?"

"This." She reached for a small black folding pen-knife and stuffed it into her front pants pocket. "And this." She grabbed the fireplace poker, gripping it with her free hand.

Nash had assumed Kiera would balk. But in the last few minutes, she'd mustered the courage he'd previously glimpsed beneath the surface. Nash wasn't sure how she'd wield the poker—or the penknife, for that matter—while balancing Heather on her hip. She hadn't put the baby down since finding the tracking device, and he doubted she would. He supposed a mother protecting her child was capable of almost anything, including brandishing a weapon. And if the fireplace poker made her feel safer, that was good enough for him.

"Your turn, Myers." The marshal hitched her thumb at the table.

Nash liked the weight and heft of the shovel. It would be awkward to carry around, however. He'd leave it by the back door and the snow shovel by the front. The baseball bat was probably a better choice for him.

"I'll take this, too." When he selected a fishing knife with a four-inch blade encased in a leather sheath, the marshal nodded approvingly. He attached the knife to his belt, then jammed a mini flashlight into his pocket. Next, he picked up the hammer and glass jar of nails he'd brought in from the shed, along with the lumber. "I'll get started on barricading the doors."

"You need help?" the marshal asked.

"I can manage."

"I'll stay with him," Kiera said and moved closer to Nash.

"Have it your way." The marshal eyed them both, though said nothing. "I'll keep watch out the front and back windows. Do you have any binoculars?"

"Mom stows a pair in the side table by the couch for bird watching."

Why hadn't he thought of the binoculars? Because he hadn't taken the danger seriously until Kiera found the tracker.

Nash mentally kicked himself. He should have mentioned his concerns about Lester earlier. But he'd let his suspicions of the marshal and catching her in a lie cloud his judgment.

"Call if you need me," the marshal said on her way to the living room.

Nash made quick work of securing the doors. He nailed three planks over both the front and mudroom doors and was regrouping in the kitchen when the marshal returned.

"I saw movement in the yard."

Nash set the hammer down on the table. "Are you sure?"

"Yes."

"Did it look like a person?" Kiera asked. She hadn't left Nash's side once.

"I can't say for certain." The marshal shifted nervously. "It might have been an animal. Is there wildlife in the area?"

"Deer," Nash said. "Elk. Coyotes. Wolves are rare, but not unheard of. They usually lay low during snowstorms."

The next second, the cabin lights went out, instantly casting them in dusk-like shadows from the sunless afternoon sky.

Kiera screamed and grabbed Nash's arm.

The marshal drew her gun.

Chapter Seven

Kiera wanted to cling to Nash and never let go, except he forced her aside in order to spring into action.

"Is the neighbor's power out, too?" the marshal asked. She'd drawn her Glock and stood at the ready.

"I can't tell." Nash moved closer to the window and stared out at twilight's dismal gray. "The trees are blocking my view. Did you bring the binoculars?"

"Here." The marshal moved her Glock to one hand and passed him the binoculars.

Kiera backed away on unsteady legs, her heart hammering painfully. She wrapped Heather in a fierce one-armed embrace, causing the baby to whimper. Before long, she'd start crying and become inconsolable.

Was that a movement in the window or Kiera's panicked imagination? She gripped the fireplace poker so hard her fingers cramped, careful to keep it far away from Heather. But she wouldn't let go of it. Not for anything.

Her thoughts raced in a dozen directions, all centered on escape. Should she put a jacket on Heather and get the baby carrier should they need to leave in a hurry? Pack bottles of formula and diapers just in case?

"Do you see anything?" she asked Nash.

"Not yet."

"What if you went upstairs?"

"Wait." He adjusted the focus. "I see lights on the hill above the treetops."

"You're positive?"

He straightened and lowered the binoculars. "Ours is the only place without power."

No need to explain the implications of that.

Chills ran up Kiera's spine. Theirs was the only place without power, and the marshal had seen movement outside.

Her thoughts scattered. The penknife! She was carrying a weapon in her pocket. Had service resumed now that the snow stopped falling? When had Heather last eaten? Kiera tried to recall her parents' phone number and couldn't. She hadn't phoned them in such a long time. Why hadn't she called her parents?

Please, dear Lord. She swallowed a sob. *Whatever happens to me, spare Heather. If I'm hurt or...if I don't survive...help my parents find their way to her. I beg You. Protect the marshal, too. And Nash. All he ever did was try to help us. He doesn't deserve to die because of me.*

"It's too much of a coincidence," the marshal said. "The power goes out shortly after we were visited by your supposed neighbor."

"Agreed." Nash tossed the binoculars onto the counter. They slid into the ceramic cookie jar with a clatter. "I'll go outside and have a look around. Maybe it's just a tripped breaker." He started for the mudroom.

"No!"

Kiera glanced around the kitchen to see who had cried out. From the stares Nash and the marshal directed at her, she'd been the source.

"I think we should all stay together," she said, striving to regain her calm. "Safety in numbers."

"It's important to know why the power's out," he said evenly, "and if we can fix it."

"What if they're out there? You'll be in danger." *Or get yourself killed.*

The marshal inclined her head in agreement. "You shouldn't stand in front of the window, Myers. Just because we can't see them, doesn't mean they can't see us."

The marshal talked as if she believed they were being watched. Kiera's nerves, already frazzled to begin with, tingled as if shot through with electricity.

"There's a path between the cluster of trees behind the shed," Nash continued. "It eventually leads to a rise that looks out onto the main road. If I take it, I should be able to see something."

"Don't go!"

Kiera was convinced if Nash went outside, he wouldn't return. That had happened once before with Joshua.

Heather began to cry. Kiera bounced the baby with her one arm, the other still clutching the fireplace poker. Refusing to be soothed, Heather continued to wail and wail. Kiera almost envied her daughter's ability to freely express herself. Kiera wanted to wail, too. That and yell at the top of her lungs.

"Please, Nash." she said. "Stay."

After a long pause, he conceded. "All right."

Relief nearly staggered her. She'd kept him safe. For now.

"I have to go upstairs," she announced. "Come with me. Both of you."

"What's upstairs?" the marshal asked.

"I need some things for Heather. Prepare for a quick departure."

"It won't come to that."

She whirled on the marshal and raised the fireplace poker. "Can you honestly say that? I found a tracking device in Heather's diaper bag. We have no idea what *it* will come to."

"Let's all go upstairs," Nash said, his tone calm yet firm. "Kiera is the one in danger. She gets to call the shots." He reached for the diaper bag on the floor.

The marshal stormed down the hall toward the stairs. "I'll go first."

They all crowded into the bedroom Kiera had been using. The marshal stood guard by the window, out of sight behind the curtains. Kiera gathered Heather's supplies while the baby rolled about on the bed under her watchful eye.

Nash, meanwhile, went through the dresser drawers and closets. He didn't say what he was looking for. Kiera and the marshal didn't inquire.

As she was transferring clean clothes from the suitcase to the diaper bag, a flicker of light caught Kiera's attention. Between his fingers, Nash dangled a small gold cross on a chain. He then stuffed the cross into his jeans pocket. When he raised his head to look at her, their gazes connected.

She nodded minutely, as if saying, "We'll take all the protection we can get."

His mouth lifted in a slight smile that had she not been looking directly at him she'd have missed. His way of saying *I'm here with you and won't leave.*

"Thank you," she whispered, confident, if he hadn't heard her, he'd read her lips.

Once again, she wished they'd met at another time, in another place. Of course, a romantic future was out of the question, but they could have been friends at least.

"I'm done," she announced and picked up Heather, along with the fireplace poker. She wasn't going anywhere without it. "We can head downstairs now."

Nash again carried the diaper bag. At the foot of the stairs, they separated. The marshal made a beeline for the living room window. Kiera and Nash, the kitchen. The intense quiet when they entered set her even more on edge. Had it been this silent before? Perhaps the difference was none of them was talking.

She changed that. "I have to warm Heather's bottle. Can you hold her?"

"I need to finish barricading the upstairs windows."

Kiera knew she should let him go, but she couldn't bear to be alone. "I don't want to put her in the baby seat on the chance…"

Nash's brows raised in surprise when she pushed the baby at him.

"I've never held a kid as young as her."

"She won't break."

Nash reluctantly took Heather.

The baby, grumpy a moment ago, instantly brightened. Her eyes went wide with interest. She wiggled her pudgy fists with excitement. Her little rosebud mouth opened in delight.

"Am I holding her the right way?" He supported her against his broad chest.

Heather lifted her hands, patted his face and cooed.

"Just right." For a second, Kiera forgot about their dire circumstances.

What if her daughter grew up never experiencing the love of a father figure? Heather had lost so much because of Joshua's actions. Kiera had forgiven him, choosing to believe he'd become entangled in a situation he couldn't escape and had lied to her solely to protect her. But it was hard sometimes to reconcile the negative impact of his choices.

And there were her frequent bouts of insomnia when she lay in bed, questioning his motives. What if she'd been a pawn all along? A means for him to keep up the appearances of a normal life and deflect suspicion away from the 7-Crowns? She'd had no chance to ask him, and the US Marshals' office wouldn't, or couldn't, give her answers.

She handed the warmed bottle to Nash. "Go on," she urged when he looked confused.

"I'm a rookie."

"It's not hard."

Heather helped by grasping the bottle and bringing it to her mouth.

"Okay." Nash nodded and appeared more confident. "I think we got it."

Kiera allowed herself to get lost in the sweet picture of Nash cuddling Heather, she content and he amused. Kiera studied every tiny detail, embedding them in her memory to enjoy later. Perhaps on those nights when she suffered insomnia. Better than dwelling on her tragic past.

The loud bang from the kitchen door didn't seem real at first, it was so out place and unexpected. At a second bang, Kiera swore the cabin walls shook.

Nash handed Kiera the baby and hollered, "Get behind me."

She did, her limbs responding instinctively to the command.

"If anything happens, take her and go to the bunker. It locks from the inside as well as the outside. No one can get in without a cannon. I'll hold them off." He reached for the baseball bat he'd left on the counter.

The bunker? "Nash, what's happening?"

But she knew the answer even before the mudroom door exploded off its hinges, the barricades Nash had nailed splintering like twigs. The man who'd called himself Lester Ahrens charged into the kitchen. Wielding an enormous handgun, he took one look at Kiera cowering behind Nash and flashed a malevolent grin that sent a wave of fear crashing through her.

"Ah. I thought I might find you here."

"Kiera!" The marshal appeared from the hallway, her Glock at the ready.

Kiera ducked farther behind Nash, shielding Heather from the anticipated gunfire exchange. Visions of the night Joshua died flashed in front of her. *Oh, dear Lord. Not again!*

But, it wasn't the same. The 7-Crowns operative was armed but this time she had a US marshal to protect her and Heather.

Kiera waited, fear cutting a jagged path through her entire body. Nash stood in front of her, a warrior primed for battle. She found a small measure of reassurance in his proximity as well as his bravery.

Only instead of the marshal firing her gun at the man, she aimed it at Kiera and Nash.

No! This couldn't be happening. Something was wrong. Terribly wrong. Kiera cowered. Surely, the marshal had a plan, and she'd act soon. Save them from this horrible man. What other explanation could there be?

"What are you doing, Gifford?" Nash shouted.

"Sorry," she said, her tone unnervingly cool. "It was never my intention to involve an outsider."

Kiera's instincts screamed at her to run, only her legs went weak and spots danced in front of her eyes. She couldn't pass out! Not now. She had to stay in control to protect Heather. Nothing else mattered except saving her helpless child.

Kiera watched, the roar from her rapid breathing filling her ears, as the man unclipped a phone from his belt. Heavier and with a thick stubby antenna, it didn't resemble any phone she'd seen before. He pressed a series of buttons before holding it to his ear. He stared directly at Kiera hovering behind Nash, his gun aimed at the pair of them.

This isn't real, her mind insisted. *It's a dream. A nightmare.* Only it was real. And there was nothing she could do to stop events from unfurling.

"I've got her," the man said into the receiver, still

grinning. "Right. Will do." He lowered the phone and addressed the marshal. "Good job. Couldn't have gotten to her without your help. Though you could've let me in earlier."

"I had no way of knowing you were from 7-Crowns and not the neighbor," she said.

"I'm here now. That's all that matters."

Kiera suddenly understood. And with that understanding came a dread like never before. Not even when she'd been hiding in her bedroom closet, convinced the men who'd killed her husband would find and kill her, too.

Marshal Gifford had betrayed her. She'd planted the tracker in the diaper bag and delivered Kiera and Heather directly into the hands of the enemy.

Abruptly, Kiera's stomach heaved. If not for cementing her teeth together, she'd have vomited all over the floor. This entire trip, perhaps from the very beginning, she'd trusted the wrong person. Now, Kiera would be paying for her mistake with her and Heather's lives. Nash's, too.

Tears flooded her eyes. Like the bile climbing her throat, she forced them back. She couldn't afford to fall apart. She needed to keep her wits about her.

"Do whatever you want with me, just please spare my daughter," she begged and squeezed Heather closer. "She's a baby. She can't identify you."

The man shrugged. "Collateral damage. Should've thought about her when you agreed to testify against The Chairman."

"Please, no."

The last word erupted from Kiera's mouth, and she

instinctively grabbed Nash's arm—the one wielding the baseball bat. It was solid enough to crack open a skull, but the man didn't appear the least bit intimidated. And why would he be? He'd shoot Nash dead before Nash took two steps.

"What are your plans?" the marshal asked the man as if she were inquiring about his day off work.

"Well, you threw a stick in the spokes when you crashed that car."

The marshal stiffened. "It was an accident."

"If not for that, our pain in the neck here and her brat would be buried under five feet of snow. Along with your partner. Guess he caught a break." The man grinned again, the movement accentuating his angular cheekbones and giving him a sinister appearance. "That blood clot could've killed him. Instead, it saved his life."

Kiera swallowed a gasp. She wasn't sure which shocked her more. That Marshal Gifford had so clearly been in communication with the 7-Crowns operative for some time or if not for the crash, Kiera and Heather would already be dead.

"How long have you been working together?" Nash asked.

He was obviously thinking along the same lines as Kiera.

The man chuckled. "Oh, Marshal Gifford and I are good friends. We were chatting regularly right up until the blizzard. Another stick in the spokes. No worries. I'm nothing if not adaptable."

Why, Kiera lamented, hadn't she left Heather at home like the Marshals' office had recommended? If only she could go back in time, her sweet girl would be safe. Instead, Kiera had stupidly played right into her adversaries' hands.

Heather's whimpering increased in volume and intensity.

"I'm not going to listen to that brat for another minute." The man's demeanor changed, all trace of false congeniality disappearing. "Where's the best place to secure them?"

"There's a bunker beneath the house," the marshal said. "It's located in the mudroom and locks from the outside."

"That should do nicely."

"What are you going to do with us?" Nash demanded.

Kiera didn't want to know.

"Get rid of you, naturally." He moved aside, his gun remaining leveled at them. "A nice drive out into the woods in the middle of the night when your nosy neighbors won't be looking. Make it look like an unfortunate accident, which happens to be my specialty. You two went searching for help on your snowmobile, took a wrong turn and got lost in the blizzard. Such a shame. And nothing to tie you to my employer."

The middle of the night. It was around five now. Which meant they had time. Hours. Not that she had the first clue how to escape. But as long as they were alive, there was hope. She had to have faith. God wouldn't desert her and Nash now when they needed Him most.

"Gifford," the man snapped, "show me the bunker."

"Back that way."

He hitched his chin at Nash and Kiera. "Move it, you two. But first, pal, lose the baseball bat."

Nash set the bat on the counter, his movements slow

and nonaggressive. "There are some jackets hanging in the mudroom. The bunker's cold."

"Like I care."

"You don't want us prematurely dying from hypothermia. That'll mess with your plans."

Kiera shivered at the thought.

The man hesitated, appearing to consider Nash's words. "Fine. Whatever. You can have some jackets. Just don't try to sneak anything in. You might lose a hand in the process."

Kiera thought of the small penknife in her pocket. Had the marshal forgotten about it in the pandemonium? Or had she even been paying attention when Kiera and Nash were selecting their makeshift weapons? Kiera couldn't remember.

Did it even matter? What good was a penknife against the man's gun?

"And some bottled water," Nash said.

The man chuckled sarcastically. "Any other requests while you're at it? A three-course meal? Some magazines?"

"Seven hours is a long time to go without water."

"Two bottles. No more."

"Thank you."

Kiera cringed at hearing Nash thank the person who intended to kill them.

She surprised herself by saying, "The diaper bag. There's formula in there and diapers."

"You're really testing my limits, lady."

The man's lethal glare caused Kiera to instantly regret her boldness, and her legs wobbled.

Nash's arm went around her waist, steadying her. "If

we went in search of help," he said, "we'd have the dia-per bag. You want our deaths to look like an accident, right? Nothing to tie them to the 7-Crowns."

How could he talk about this so calmly?

Rather than answer, the man growled at the marshal. "Look through the bag. Remove anything they might use to pick the lock."

She holstered her gun and did as he instructed, thor-oughly inspecting each pocket and compartment. She removed the remaining diaper pins, a ballpoint pen and several of Heather's toys. "That's it."

"You sure?"

"Positive." She straightened and stepped away.

The man kicked the diaper bag toward Nash and Kiera. It made an ominous scraping sound as it slid across the floor, stopping a few inches short of Nash. He bent and picked it up. "The water's in the fridge."

The man's eyes narrowed to slits. "You don't know when to stop, do you?"

"You promised us two bottles."

He angled his head toward the marshal. "Get their water. Give 'em three while you're at it. I'm feeling gen-erous." He chuckled again.

"What about some food?" Nash asked.

"You're joking."

Kiera admired his daring in the face of adversity. On the other hand, she worried he'd go too far, and the man's temper would explode. Then what? He'd put a bullet in their heads.

The marshal retrieved the water bottles from the re-frigerator. She didn't immediately hand them to Nash. Rather, she tucked them beneath her arm.

Strange and scary. Then it hit Kiera. The marshal was keeping her distance from the 7-Crowns operative. Because of fear? Caution? To stay out of the way of any potential gunfire? All of the above?

"You first, Marshal," the man singsonged, his smirk back in place. "Lead the way."

She did. Kiera reluctantly followed and then Nash, the man's gun tracking their every move. Kiera hugged Heather to her, shielding her baby's face when they passed the man. She felt his gaze cover her like a coating of slime. It made her desperate to flee.

In the mudroom, Nash set down the diaper bag. He then grabbed two coats and two jackets from the hooks on the wall. Ignoring the man's impatient scowl, he added three knitted caps and several scarves to the pile.

"Go through everything," the man barked at the marshal.

Again, she complied, removing a set of keys from one of the coats and tossing them into a corner.

"Now, search them."

Kiera gulped. Nash stood agonizingly still.

The marshal patted them down, Nash first and then Kiera. She found and removed their phones from their pockets, shoving them into her jacket. Kiera almost yelped when the marshal's fingers skimmed over the penknife. She kept her mouth shut, however, and the marshal's fingers moved to the next spot.

How had she missed the knife? And what about the one Nash carried? Why blatantly defy the man?

"Good." He looked down. "Now open the trapdoor."

The marshal knelt, unfastened the lock and yanked open the heavy trapdoor leading to the bunker. The hinges creaked loudly from lack of use. A gust of frigid air shot out, filling every corner of the room. She struggled to her feet and then retreated until her back touched the wall.

No doubt about it. She was afraid of the man.

"We need light," Nash said with that same incredible calm.

"Scared of the dark?" The operative chuckled.

"There's a battery-operated lantern on the shelf there."

"Get it," he barked at the marshal.

She handed Nash the lantern. He pressed a button, and when its dim light bulb illuminated, he held the lantern over the opening.

Kiera saw a very narrow set of stairs and tensed. How was she supposed to climb down there with Heather? She'd fall and break a leg.

"Is that a rope?" The man was looking through the small window between the mudroom and the carport. "Go grab it," he told the marshal.

"You're not going to tie us up." Nash placed himself between the man and Kiera. "There's no need. We can't escape the bunker."

No longer able to suppress her emotions, Kiera blurted, "My baby. Don't do this to her."

"Not you two," the man grumbled in disgust. "I can't have the medical examiner finding any marks on your bodies." He indicated the marshal. "The rope's for her."

"What are you talking about?" The marshal's composure wavered. "I'm going with you."

"There's been a change of plans."

"I don't understand."

"You'll corroborate the story that our girl here and

her boyfriend left on their own while you stayed behind in case help arrived, taking the heat off my employer when their bodies are found. If you don't cooperate…" He shrugged. "You know what will happen."

"Why tie me up?" Her hand fluttered to her throat, the gesture uncharacteristic.

"You're unreliable. You destroyed the tracker. And you called your son when you were given strict orders to contact no one."

"How do you—"

"We're not stupid," the man continued, "and we can't take the chance you go all soft and double-cross us. I'll untie you when we're ready to leave."

"You need my help," she protested.

"No, I don't. Reinforcements are on the way."

Kiera didn't like the sound of that.

"Now quit your stalling and get the rope," he snapped.

Uncertainty crossed the marshal's face. Uncertainty and, Kiera was sure of it, defiance. For a few desperate moments, she hoped the marshal might draw her Glock and take charge of the situation.

Only, she didn't. And by going into the carport for the rope, she may well have sealed all their fates, including her own.

Chapter Eight

Nash dropped the bundle of outerwear through the open trapdoor. It tumbled to the bottom of the stairs. The three bottles of water were next, along with the diaper bag and the battery-operated lantern. They needed much more, but he didn't ask. The 7-Crowns operative would say no and might even take out his anger on them.

"I'll go first," Nash told Kiera. The raw fear blazing in her eyes cut him clear to his core. There was nothing he wanted more than to erase it. And he could. Maybe.

But not right now with the 7-Crowns operative's gun pointed at him. Besides, he didn't want to raise her hopes only to dash them. He had no idea if the old tunnel leading to the shed was still navigable or if it had collapsed again. "You hand Heather to me. I won't drop her, I promise."

Kiera just stood there, her lips trembling, her head slowly shaking no.

"It's okay, hon."

He refused to believe they were soon to spend their last hours on Earth. Yet, if their one and only chance failed them, they wouldn't see morning's glorious light or their families' faces again.

God, please. Grant me the courage to endure what's to come and the ability to save us if I can. I'm confident of what awaits me in Your heavenly kingdom, but I'm honest enough to admit getting there scares me a little. It scares Kiera, too. She and Heather shouldn't have to pay with their lives for witnessing her husband's murder.

Feeling the Lord's strength flow into him, he pivoted and carefully lowered himself down the bunker's steps. Cold air seeped through his jeans and shirt, chilling his skin with icy fingers. He stopped, his head just above the opening, and breathed deeply.

He could do this. He *had* to do this. Kiera and Heather were depending on him. He wasn't sure how they'd escape even if the tunnel was still accessible, but he wouldn't sit in a bunker and helplessly await their fate.

"How dare you betray me!"

Nash's head shot up. The accusation Kiera flung at Marshal Gifford startled him with its force. Fury ignited her every word.

"I trusted you," she continued. "The Marshals' office trusted you. The prosecution. A murderer will go free and more people will die because of you. Not just me and Heather and Nash. Countless others. You've made everything I sacrificed for worth nothing."

"I had no choice," the marshal said.

"There's always a choice."

"They have my son and daughter under surveillance." She faltered. "Day and night. They send me videos showing me just how close they are."

"You have a daughter, too? What else haven't you told me? Did you intentionally crash the car into that tree?"

Nash had been wondering the same thing.

"The syndicate's threatened to kill my children if I don't cooperate." Her gaze cut briefly to the operative. "And you know better than anyone that the 7-Crowns carries out their threats."

"I'm getting bored, ladies," the man said with a snarl.

"Heather is just a baby." Kiera laid her cheek on the top of her daughter's head, her voice breaking. "How can you let them kill her?"

"How can I let them kill my son and daughter? I'm in a position no one should ever be in." The fight drained from the marshal, and her features crumbled. "I don't expect you to understand or forgive me. Just know I would never have forsaken you and Heather or my duty for any other reason."

Nash hadn't liked the marshal from the beginning. In this moment, however, he empathized with her. What would he do if he had to choose between saving his children or someone else? Would he be able to live with whichever decision he made? He prayed God showed the marshal some mercy, for she'd been placed in an unconscionable position.

"Enough bellyaching." The operative reached for Kiera with the hand not holding the gun and gave her a rough shove toward the bunker door. "Get down there before I throw you down."

He would, too. Nash had no doubt.

"Give me Heather." He reached up. When Kiera wavered, he said, "I've got her. And you."

She looked at him with agony and despair, and he guessed it was more for Heather than herself. She'd do anything to save her daughter.

"We're going to get through this. Have faith."

"Give him the ankle biter or I will," the man bellowed, his patience used up.

Kiera did. Arms shaking, she passed Heather to Nash. He grabbed the crying baby around the waist and laid her over his shoulder. He then descended the remaining distance to the bunker floor, one careful step at a time. He wouldn't drop his tiny charge. At the bottom, he surveyed his surroundings in the lantern's dim light. Thankfully, the bulb hadn't burned out.

He stepped over the diaper bag and pile of clothes and set the lantern on the table. Next, he bent and tossed the rest of the stuff aside. Heather began to cry, probably from the cold and the musty stale smell. She also wasn't used to an unfamiliar man bouncing her around.

Kiera's voice traveled down to Nash. "I'll pray for your souls."

"Don't waste your breath," came a gruff reply.

A moment later, her feet appeared at the top of the stairs. The old steps squeaked in protest. As she neared the bottom, he gripped her elbow to steady her.

Without warning, the trapdoor slammed shut, the noise like a cannon shot. It was Kiera's undoing, and she crumpled. Nash caught her before her knees gave out and pulled her to him, hugging her and Heather. Kiera buried her face in his shirt and broke into gutwrenching sobs. Heather's crying increased.

"Shh." He stroked Kiera's back in the way he'd seen her comfort her daughter. "Don't cry, hon."

She wrapped an arm around his neck. "I don't want to die. Not like this. My poor parents. I haven't seen them since right before I went into witness protection and I've only talked to them twice. They've never met Heather. And now they never will." She raised desperate eyes to his. "What if they blame me? They begged me not to testify, but I insisted."

"They won't blame you. None of this is your fault."

Kiera appeared not to hear him. "I should have left Heather at home. Why didn't I? I knew the syndicate was after me. I was warned. Repeatedly."

Nash's commitment to save her and Heather increased tenfold. "You believed you both were safe in the custody of a US marshal. Anyone would."

She shuddered, from cold and shock and fear and maybe even disbelief. She hadn't expected Gifford to betray her. The woman was a US marshal. Presumed to be dedicated to serving the public.

"I'm so sorry I dragged you into this," she said, her shivering escalating.

"You didn't." Nash blamed himself. He'd fallen for the man's bogus story. He must have taken the chance Mrs. Smithson hadn't yet met the real Lester Ahrens, either, and fooled her when he visited. How else could he have known what to say to convincingly pass himself off an imposter?

"You must hate me," Kiera lamented.

"Far from it."

"But I—"

"We're going to get out of here."

"We'll need a miracle," she said, utterly defeated.

For a second, just one, Nash was tempted to surrender as well. Let go and let God, as the saying went. It was how his mother dealt with her MS.

But unlike her, he believed God helped those who helped themselves. He'd blessed Nash with two strong arms, a brain and a heart filled with determination. He'd want Nash to use his abilities to find a way out of their predicament.

"He giveth power to the faint; and to them that have no might He increaseth strength."

"What did you say?" Kiera stopped crying and wiped her nose with the back of her hand.

"I think it's from Isaiah. I don't remember the exact verse. Our minister says that God has given us what we need. We just have to delve inside ourselves and find it."

She nodded and sniffed again, more composed than a moment ago.

Heather, too, had quieted. She'd stuffed her thumb in her mouth and snuggled her head in the crook of Nash's neck. Without thinking, he patted her back.

"Since yesterday," he said, "I've been questioning what purpose God had in bringing us together. I think it's that you and Heather needed an ally against the marshal and the 7-Crowns operative."

"Oh, Nash." Rather than lean more into him, Kiera stood a little straighter and took Heather from him. "As much as I'm glad to not be alone, I hate that you're involved."

"Kiera, listen carefully." He walked them away from the stairs. "There may be a way to get out of here, but we don't have any time to waste."

Uncertainty, mingled with hope, flashed in her eyes. "We can escape?"

"Possibly."

"How?"

"There's a tunnel."

"A tunnel!"

"It's in the bathroom. There's a panel in the back of the storage closet." Even as he told her, he worried if he'd be able to open the tunnel door without proper tools. Or, much worse, come face-to-face with a wall of dirt and rocks.

"Where does it lead?" she asked, her shivering abating.

"To the shed behind the cabin. We were told the original owners stored guns and ammunition in the tunnel."

"My God. Nash, we can get away."

"It's not that simple," he cautioned. "The tunnel may have collapsed. It's been over twenty years since anyone's used it. Back then, we had to excavate it, which took days with picks and shovels."

"We have to try."

"I agree. And once we reach the shed, we can take the snowmobile."

Her face lit up. "I forgot about that."

"We still need to make a plan," Nash cautioned. "The snowmobile will make a loud noise when I start it. That can't be helped. They'll hear it in the cabin. He drove here in some sort of all-terrain vehicle that's probably parked nearby, and I guarantee he'll come after us."

Kiera didn't allow his warning to tarnish her excitement. "But we can get away. We don't have to go far. Just to a neighbor's house."

"No. I don't want to endanger someone by bringing a killer to their door."

"Where then?"

"I'm not sure yet," Nash said. "I have to think. And none of that will matter if the tunnel's collapsed."

"Let's look!"

She grabbed his hand. Their current dire circumstances made no difference. Her slim fingers felt right in his, and he didn't want to let go—and wouldn't have if getting out alive wasn't their first, and only, priority.

"We will. After we put on warm clothes. Heather's cold, and we have to conserve our energy. Especially since we have no food."

"We do. Baby food."

"Save my share for Heather."

"There's plenty."

Together, they sorted through the pile of clothing, donning double layers of coats and jackets. Nash set the bottles of water on the old table. Kiera changed Heather's diaper and then zipped her inside her large coat, warming her daughter further with her body heat. With Heather secured and more or less comfortable, she offered the baby a bottle of cold formula from the diaper bag, which initially Heather refused but then accepted.

Nash stuffed caps on his and Kiera's heads and wound scarves around their necks. Kiera put the third and smallest cap on Heather. The added warmth and having a possible means of escape restored their spirits some. In Heather's case, it was having a full tummy that did the trick.

Kiera's eyes sought Nash's, and when they met, he nodded and gave her cap a tug. A small gesture that meant more than she could express. After a moment, she broke away.

"Why do you think the marshal let us keep our knives?"

"Guilt?" Nash suggested. "So she can convince herself she didn't leave us entirely defenseless and is able to sleep at night?"

"You're probably right. Plus, she knows the operative will be guarding the trapdoor. We won't use the knives to jimmy the lock."

"If by some miracle we escape through the tunnel, and the operative discovers we're gone, he'll hunt us down. And he won't care about making it look like an accident."

She thought a moment before answering. "If I have to die, I want to die trying to get away. Not just sitting here, doing nothing."

He didn't argue.

Glancing around the bunker, he said, "I think best when I'm working. Let's check the tunnel opening first. If it's blocked, and we can't reach the shed, we won't need to worry about the operative and Gifford coming after us. After that, we'll go through the cupboards. Look for anything useful. I don't care if it's a shoelace or a paperclip. Put whatever you find on the table. By then, I should have a plan."

Kiera didn't understand how it was possible, but Heather slept while she searched the bunker. Of course, her little baby didn't understand the gravity of their situation. Thank God. At least she'd be spared the horror of their potential impending demises.

Exhaustion also accounted for her ability to nap. Kiera herself was too agitated to think about sleeping. Even if the three of them survived this ordeal—no, *when* they survived this ordeal—she'd probably never enjoy a good night's slumber for the rest of her life. Every time she closed her eyes, she would remember this day, and the paralyzing fear.

Nash alone was responsible for her being able to function. His support and her determination to save her daughter.

Kiera had begun her search with the floor-to-ceiling cabinets. From there, she inspected an old footlocker and the vanity in the tumbledown bathroom with its faded paint, dingy fixtures and sagging ceiling.

Needing freedom of movement, and restricted by Heather snuggled against her, Kiera had eventually shrugged off her outer coat, wrapped the baby inside it and nestled her in the now-empty footlocker for the remainder of her nap. Every five minutes, less sometimes, she'd stop what she was doing and check on Heather, who was always dozing peacefully. Amazing. Really.

Kiera had found a handful of loose change, a moth-eaten skein of yarn, a grungy pair of old slippers, some paperclips, a button, three Lego pieces and enough rat droppings and dead bugs to turn her stomach. The only item of any use was a five-inch screwdriver she'd discovered in a corner behind the table.

Nash had struggled to pry open the three-by-three-foot panel in the bathroom linen closet that hid the tunnel. Lying on his side, he'd pushed steadily with the soles of his feet until his knees shook violently from the strain. Kiera had been little help. He'd tried using the knives, only to quit before bending the blades.

When she'd showed him the screwdriver, he grunted his approval. Using the pointed end, he'd dug around the edges of the panel, not stopping even when his palms started to bleed. Eventually, he'd been able to loosen whatever gummy substance had caused the panel to stick like glue. The next time he'd pushed at the panel with his feet, it gave with a crack and fell into the tunnel opening.

Air colder than that in the bunker had blasted them in the face and triggered a wave of excitement followed by apprehension. Air meant the tunnel hadn't collapsed. It also meant that Kiera would have to crawl fifty yards through a dark narrow, filthy and icy cold passage filled with small animals and insects and reptiles lying dormant for the winter.

But it was their only way out, and there was nothing she wouldn't do for Heather. God would be there beside them, guiding their way.

Currently, Nash was on all fours, the top half of his body inside the tunnel. He'd explained that the tunnel ran eight to ten feet below ground level, the same depth as the bunker floor. When they reached the shed, there would be a chute leading straight up that they'd need to climb.

He scooted out of the tunnel and sat back on his calves, the battery-operated lantern in his hand.

"Is something wrong?" Kiera asked.

He fished in his pocket. "Just getting the flashlight. The light from the lantern only projects in a small circle."

She'd forgotten about the flashlight. Thankfully, the

marshal hadn't taken it. Would she have if she'd known about the tunnel?

Standing behind Nash, she watched him direct the flashlight into the tunnel. The beam didn't reach far, a few feet at most. All Kiera saw was empty blackness.

Above them, footsteps sounded. They'd heard them off and on. At first, the noise alarmed them. Eventually, they'd grown accustomed to the operative traipsing through the cabin, doing whatever it was he was doing. Plotting their demise, no doubt.

Nash returned to the tunnel, crawling in farther than before. All but his shoes disappeared. Several minutes later, he inched out, his outerwear and cap covered in dirt.

"What do you see?" Kiera asked, trying not to get her hopes too high.

Twisting sideways, he sat on the floor. Exhaustion shadowed his handsome features. Opening the panel had sapped his strength. Would he have enough left to reach the shed and then whatever lay ahead? Kiera couldn't make it on her own.

"It looks clear."

"Good." She released a long breath.

"For as far as I can see, which isn't more than thirty feet ahead. We could get halfway to the shed and find a wall of dirt. Then we'd have to turn around and come back."

She didn't want to think about that outcome.

"I could crawl ahead while you and Heather wait here. Then come back for you."

"No. That would take too much time. And I don't want you going anywhere without us." Kiera's hopes deflated only to rise again. "What if we hide in the tunnel? We could put the panel in place behind us."

Nash stood, dislodging dirt particles and sending then to the floor in a small shower. "We wouldn't last long. Heather especially. Not without blankets. Besides, it wouldn't take the operative long to find us. The trapdoor is locked from the outside. He'd realize we had to be somewhere in the bunker and eventually find the panel, especially with Gifford's help. You can rest assured he'll untie her if he realizes we're missing. Not to mention the reinforcements. We have no idea when they're arriving."

"You're right."

"I'm also worried the operative won't wait until the middle of the night."

Kiera bit her lower lip to stop herself from breaking apart. Obstacles faced them at every turn.

"I'm willing to take the chance the tunnel is clear," Nash said. "If you are."

She nodded. "What other choice do we have?"

He put an arm around her. "Let's sit at the table. I need to rest. Plus, we should drink some water and eat a little food."

"There's applesauce and vanilla wafers in the diaper bag."

"My favorite. We can finalize our game plan over lunch."

She liked his stab at humor. It eased some of her nervousness. As did his arm on her shoulders when he led her to the table. The heavy, but not proprietary, weight made her feel safe and cared for.

Was she fooling herself? Allowing their circumstances to affect her emotions? Kiera had been duped before. By Joshua. Marshal Gifford. Two people she'd trusted implicitly. Who was to say it wouldn't happen again with Nash? She hardly knew him. He was almost a stranger.

Just as they were sitting down at the rickety table, Heather awoke from her nap with a loud cry. Kiera changed her diaper and then dug through the diaper bag for food while Nash balanced the baby on his lap.

When she clasped his finger in her chubby fist, he smiled. "Hey, kiddo. Hungry?"

Heather gurgled and gave him a drooly smile.

Nash used his coat sleeve to wipe her mouth. She doubted the lack of a proper baby wipe would hurt either of them.

She paused, listening to her heart. *How could you think you don't know him? Just look at them.*

Smiling, Kiera set an unopened jar of applesauce on the table and a sleeve of vanilla wafers.

"Feast for a king," Nash said, a smile in his voice.

"Wish I had a couple of sandwiches instead."

"This is fine." He balanced Heather against his arm as he unscrewed the lid from the applesauce jar.

Kiera produced two baby spoons.

Nash held his up for inspection. "I'd be laughing under different circumstances."

"I'll share my spoon with Heather."

Kiera opened the last jar of strained chicken and carrots. Heather also needed to refuel before their adventure. Who knew when they'd next have an opportunity to eat?

Nash continued holding Heather, enabling Kiera to

feed her. In between, he and Kiera ate their meager meal. She wasn't hungry but forced herself to swallow. Keeping warm burned a lot of calories.

"I've been running through our options," Nash said, scooping a mini spoonful of applesauce from the jar and taking a bite. "Once we're on the snowmobile, we'll drive to the gas station. Henry Joe lives in an apartment above the shop. He's always there."

"I thought you said you didn't want to endanger any innocent people."

"I don't. But Henry Joe is a retired police detective. The garage is like Fort Knox. He'll recognize me and let us in."

"Assuming the operative and marshal and any reinforcements don't catch up with us."

"Assuming," Nash agreed. "Henry Joe also has a two-way radio. Even if phone service is still out, he can reach someone. And the garage isn't far, less than two miles if we cut through the woods."

She pressed a hand to her chest and felt her racing heartbeat. "I'm scared, Nash. Really scared."

"I am, too."

The moment wasn't lost on her. Here she sat, her life on the line, with a man she'd met only two days ago, now bouncing her baby on his lap. She should be screaming at the top of her lungs at the unfairness of it all. Or huddling in a corner, begging God to spare them. Instead, she watched Nash and Heather together and garnered a tiny shred of peace.

"Finish up," he said and scraped the last spoonful from his jar. "It's time for us to make our move."

Chapter Nine

"Are you okay?" Nash cranked his head around as far as the cramped space would allow.

"Yes."

Kiera's dim form appeared a few feet behind him. Only her eyes were clearly visible. The rest of her blended into the darkness.

"You sure?"

"Let's keep moving."

Her lackluster response didn't reassure him. There was, however, nothing he could do. They had to continue.

He'd carry her and Heather on his back through the tunnel if it were possible, but there was barely enough room to accommodate him on all fours. With each forward movement, his shoulders brushed the sides and roof of the tunnel, dislodging loose dirt and small pebbles that fell into his eyes and covered his face.

His skin itched. His knees ached. His palms stung from constant scraping along the cold hard ground. It must be ten times worse for Kiera, who carried Heather bundled inside her jacket.

Unbelievably, the baby wasn't crying. Neither was Kiera. That she held herself together under such harrowing circumstances impressed Nash. Like him, though, she was tired and they moved slowly. Their pace was further hampered by Nash having to aim the mini flashlight ahead of them. Beyond the meager beam, vast nothingness loomed, blacker than midnight.

"How's Heather doing?" he asked, creeping forward. In addition to the pain, his fingers were numb from the cold.

"She's okay."

"What about you? How are *you* doing?"

"Is it much farther?"

Staring ahead, Nash tried to visualize the tunnel's end and the shed's location to the cabin. They'd traveled roughly halfway. "Twenty-five yards or so."

It had taken them nearly an hour to travel this distance. At their current rate, and by Nash's calculations, they'd reach their destination at around 8:00 p.m. Assuming the tunnel remained clear. With each foot they journeyed, more bits of the roof showered down on them. If it collapsed, they'd be trapped and expire from lack of oxygen long before hypothermia set in.

"Eeek!"

At Kiera's squeal of fright and frantic scuffling, Nash halted. "What's wrong?"

"Something ran across my leg."

"Probably a mouse or a mole."

"Not a snake?"

"They become lethargic in cold weather."

"How lethargic?"

"I wouldn't worry." Not about that. "Is the mouse gone now?"

"I think so."

He gave her another few seconds to collect herself. "You okay now?"

"Yeah."

"You're doing great, hon."

"God gives us no more than we can handle, right?" The forced bravado in her tone didn't mask her fear.

"You've been through a lot recently. And you've dealt amazingly well with it."

"I have been through a lot all year. And not always dealt well with it."

He resumed crawling, glad when he heard the sound of her slow shuffling behind him. She hadn't quit, not that he thought she would. "Are you able to talk about it?"

"Now? Seriously?"

"Conversation might help pass the time and take our minds off stuff."

"Stuff like we could be buried under ten tons of dirt at any moment?"

"I was thinking of mice."

"Funny. Not."

She had a point, though. What would happen to them if Nash's plan didn't work? He visualized God's mighty hand holding up the tunnel roof until they reached the end.

He pushed away images of the operative and Gifford waiting for them at the shed, guns drawn. Positive thoughts only, he told himself.

"Other than my parents, Joshua's parents and law

enforcement, I haven't spoken to anyone about what happened the night of Joshua's cold-blooded murder," Kiera said. "Just the police, the FBI and the US Marshals. Oh, and the county prosecutor."

She hadn't put her late husband's death in those terms before, and Nash was glad she couldn't see his face. He'd never met anyone whose loved one had been killed in such a terrible manner. Poor Kiera. Poor Heather. "I'm so sorry."

"It happened in our backyard." She grunted as she struggled to talk and keep pace with him. "I saw the whole thing through our second-story bedroom window."

"You don't have to tell me, Kiera, if you'd rather not." Nash glanced backward. Her pale features stood out stark white against their surroundings.

"Actually, I want to tell you. I've been coping with this alone for a long time, and it's wearing on me. Not that I want to burden you with my troubles."

"You're not burdening me. I want to know more about you. But only if the telling doesn't distress you."

She said nothing for several moments. Nash assumed she'd changed her mind, but then she suddenly restarted her story—haltingly at first, and then with growing conviction. As they progressed through the tunnel, inch by painstaking inch, he listened. That was all he could do. Her poignant and horrifying tale left him at a loss for words.

"Joshua was a CPA with a reputable accounting firm. Smart. Charming. Sweet. Churchgoing. From a big family. Everything I wanted in man, and we fell head over at risk of encountering other obstacles or meeting up with the killers."

She blew out a shaky breath. "Tomorrow it is. I can't guarantee how far I can go, but I'll try."

He handed Josiah back to her. "We'll do what you can, but for now, you need to eat. How about the last apple and another trail mix?"

"Sounds good." He started out of the tent, and she grabbed his hand. "Thank you again for taking care of us. You could've already been home by now."

"Wouldn't have it any other way." He disappeared outside the tent with Rex on his heels.

She took in a deep breath and released it slowly. "I can do this. I can finish this journey," she whispered. "Lord, Your Word says I can do all things through You, and You'll give me strength. I need all the strength I can get. Thank You for answering my prayer, and thank You for my healthy baby."

Trent leaned inside and handed her the snacks along with a bottled water. "Drink all the water. You need it. I'll boil water from the waterfall in the coffee pot and refill our empty bottles."

"You can do that? Is it safe?"

"Yep. Boil three minutes and let it cool. May take the rest of the afternoon to get them refilled, but I'll get it done." He slipped back out.

Brooke munched on the apple and trail mix. Could she ever eat them again without the reminder of this day? She splashed a little of the water from her bottle on her face and sipped on the rest. She longed for a shower and her pillow top mattress.

Weariness washed over her. She lay on her side with Josiah snug against her chest and closed her eyes.

Water splashing woke her. She raised up and peered outside the tent. What was Trent doing standing in the river? He held a long stick and threw it into the water. Pulled it out and waited, then threw it in again. When he lifted it up again, a fish was on the other end. He'd speared a fish.

Admiration for his survival skills amazed her. Enjoying a fish dinner made her mouth water. The protein would help give her extra strength needed to begin the next trek through the woods.

She forced herself to her feet and emerged from the tent, holding Josiah. Trent stepped out of the water and walked toward her, holding his catch in the air, smiling.

"Thought I'd try my hand at spear fishing." He laughed. "Had to improvise since I abandoned all my gear back at the camp. It worked. We have two trout. Who knew? Tonight, we're having a feast."

"You actually speared a fish. I can hardly wait to sink my teeth into something besides crackers and trail mix." She kissed Josiah's head.

"Gotta clean them. The propane tank is running low on fuel. I'm going to cook these on our small fire."

"What do you need me to do?" How could she help with her body feeling drained?

"Nothing. Maybe walk around and work up some strength for tomorrow's hike." He popped out his knife and tossed the fish on a rock. "Relax and enjoy Josiah. I've got this."

His cell phone was lying on top of his backpack. He'd changed the cover photo to the selfie he took of the four of them. Josiah, Rex, himself and her. She couldn't help but smile. So much stress had dissolved today, and her fear of childbirth no longer terrified her.

She strolled to the water's edge and walked closer to the waterfall. A fine mist moistened her face. She covered Josiah's head with the blanket and enjoyed the beauty of her surroundings.

"Mom, I'll be home soon, and you can meet your grandson," she whispered. "No one will ever believe my story. I'm uncertain how the birth certificate will read. Smoky Mountain waterfall baby? Born in the wild?"

Would she ever return here? Maybe. Depending on whether search and rescue located them before the killers. Her pulse increased. She couldn't think about that. No one would ever take her baby away from her.

She searched the tree line above. Amazingly, she hadn't broken a bone or hurt Josiah when she fell. Were those men up there watching? No gunshots, so evidently, they didn't know where to look.

Her little bundle squirmed. She patted his back and swayed, cuddling him close to her chest. So dainty and fragile. Her responsibilities now changed forever. Caring and nurturing took on a whole new meaning. Getting him home to his newly decorated room added another hurdle to her agenda.

The smell of smoke tickled her nose. She spun. Trent sat by the fire, cooking the fish. She sauntered her way back to the camp and inspected the open-air roasting. Two forked sticks stuck in the ground on each side of the flames. The two long sticks, holding both fish, rested on the forked ones. His resourceful abilities impressed her again.

"You never cease to amaze me."

"Oh, nothing to it." He poked the fire. "Camping survival books explain how to do everything, well, except deliver babies in the wild. Our dinner is almost ready."

"I'm glad you did your homework. And I'm glad you trusted God to help you through your situation. He helped me see that anything is possible with Him. I was caught up in feelings of rejection and betrayal and had determined I couldn't trust myself to make important decisions."

He stilled and looked at her. "Glad you've found breakthrough. Seems He knocked down a few bricks in my thinking, too. The sergeant will be glad I'm showing signs of improvement. I'm certain he's lining up a lot of overtime for me. He knows I love my job and I'd work twenty-four hours a day if needed."

She broke eye contact. Needn't pursue her admiration of him. His love was his job with no room for her. She longed for someone to share her and her son's life with, not a workaholic.

Her tastebuds came to life with the first bite. She'd never been so hungry for actual food, and the natural flavor tasted like a delicacy. No salt, no spices. Meat only. Trent shared some of his fish with Rex, then gave him another packet of dog food and a snack. He made camping look fun, but then, he hadn't trudged up a mountain thirty-eight weeks pregnant and had a baby. Maybe, minus those hurdles, the adventure wouldn't be as dreadful.

"Can't believe I ate the whole thing, well, except for the bones." She licked her fingers. "Delicious."

"We needed something solid. Hiking takes a lot out

of you." He took the bones to the edge of the cliff wall and buried them. "Easy cleanup. I suggest you get as much rest as you can tonight. We have a long day tomorrow."

"Do you think anyone's reported us missing yet?" Her thoughts swirled. "My parents are probably beside themselves with worry."

"Since I haven't reported in, my parents know something's not right. I'm confident they've already called the ranger's station." He reached over and squeezed her hand. "We are going to make it. I expect sometime tomorrow help will arrive."

"You really think so?" His assurance encouraged her. Anticipation mounted. She looked to the sky. "Thank You for watching over us, Lord. Send help soon."

Daylight dwindled and darkness fell over the camp. Josiah wiggled and squirmed. His squeaky cry grew louder.

"Guess I'd better feed him and turn in for the night. Thank you for the fish. Maybe all of us will get some rest." She walked over to the opening of the tent and paused. She turned and faced him. "Thank you, Trent, for everything. I couldn't have made it without you. You're a godsend and I really appreciate your honesty and courage."

Trent pushed to his feet and walked toward her. His gaze bored into hers. He pulled her close. "I should be thanking you. My life has taken on a new meaning since I met you. I'm not wallowing in my failures and dreading Josiah's delivery."

He looked down at her with the tiny bundle and

couldn't help himself. His hands cupped her cheeks as he leaned in and kissed her soft lips.

She placed her hand against his chest, pushed back and stared at him with a questioning look. Her lips parted, but he placed his finger over them.

"Congratulations. You amaze me. You and Josiah get some rest." Could she feel the hard beats thudding against his chest? She'd captured his heart without trying. He turned back toward the campfire. Her warm hand gripped his arm.

"I know you're a K-9 handler in search and rescue and birthing babies isn't in your job description, but you managed today like a pro, with intelligence and compassion and for the record, his full name is Josiah Trent Chandler. I'm naming him after the one who rescued us in this wilderness and brought him into the world. We will never forget you."

He fought tears. It wasn't like him to get emotional. Not like this. He never expected her to name Josiah after him. His eyes, once again, bored into her gentle, caring gaze. "Don't know what to say, except I'm honored."

"And I'm forever grateful."

He kissed her again on the lips and turned back to the campfire before his emotions got the best of him. Rex curled up beside him on the ground. He ran fingers through the soft fur and stared into the blaze. He'd heard of love at first sight, but he never saw himself in this situation. It wasn't at first sight for him, but he *had* found her attractive, just hadn't expected to develop feelings overnight.

Had he been so overjoyed by a safe delivery and healthy baby that he'd lost his senses and thought he had feelings for her? He gave Rex a treat. Brooke. He couldn't get her off his mind, and yet, she'd just commented she'd never forget him like being rescued would end their relationship. Her soft lips molded perfectly against his. Had he been presumptuous?

He'd made himself available at work for extended hours since he lived alone and had nothing better to do. Attraction to Brooke had him rethinking his hours and his future with a ready-made family. She'd participated in both kisses, so it wasn't one-sided. Was it? Mixed emotions ate at him.

He slid down closer to the fire and stared at the sky until his eyes grew heavy. Getting them out of these mountains without encountering more danger was a priority. However, Zeke and the two other nameless men, he assumed, were still on the hunt. He and Brooke had chanced a fire two nights in a row. Would they spot the campfire and stray from the main trail in search of them? Would Josiah's cry draw them closer? His gut twisted.

Lord, could You keep those guys away and send help tomorrow?

Early dawn came too soon. An idea popped into Trent's head. He dug into the backpack and pulled out his one extra pair of jeans and extra shirt. Opened the first aid kit and snagged the small scissors. He could hardly wait to see the surprise on her face when she saw what he'd made.

Rex bounced around, racing up and down the riverbank. Trent picked up a stick and tossed it. "Fetch." He chased after it and brought it back. "Good boy. Have a treat. These are your favorites."

Rex barked.

"Shhh, quiet. You'll wake her."

He glanced inside the open space of the tent. Brooke sat quietly, looking down at her baby. Her baby. She was a mother now. Her hand smoothed over his blond hair, circled her finger around his small ears, and she kissed those soft cheeks.

How could he invade her private moment? So serene. So momentous. Had he ever taken the time to capture such delicate moments? The love she displayed captivated him. He looked away. Rex nudged his hand.

"These will make her happy, Rex. We'll be back home before you know it."

Brooke emerged from the tent with her bundle, no bigger than a football, wrapped up in Mandy's doll blanket. "Good morning."

"You're awake. Hope you got some rest."

"I slept well, except for feeding times." She stepped closer and looked at the strips of cloth lying across his backpack. "What are these?"

"May not be perfect, but I made some diapers out of the only clean shirt I had left, and I made one of those sling things from my last pair of jeans. My sister had one with Mandy, so I figured it would come in handy today."

He held up small, square pieces of fabric with ripped corners. "Tie them on with these."

Her jaw dropped. "You're going to make me cry. How thoughtful and clever. I am blown away."

His chest swelled. He had impressed her.

"Thank you so much. I didn't know what I was going to do!" She laughed.

"And look." He held up the length of his denim jeans with the legs cut open. The ends were slit like the diapers. The sling was a little smaller than normal ones but should work.

"I love it. Your ingenuity amazes me. Tie it around me and let's see how it works." She held Josiah up against her chest.

He stood in front of her and put the center of the fabric under Josiah's body, then looped it up around her neck and tied it. The second leg went around her abdomen and he fastened it in the back.

"How does that feel?" He stepped away and lifted his eyebrows.

She walked around and bounced a little. "Feels fantastic. Tighten it a little more and it will be perfect. I think you've just invented the emergency baby wrap."

She threw her arms around his neck and hugged him. "Thank you."

The warmth of her embrace messed with his emotions. She tried stepping back, but he didn't want this moment to end. He held her a little longer. Was he getting too involved? Were his feelings mounting because she'd forced him to face his fears?

"I'm happy if you are." He kissed her forehead and turned away. "Take a few minutes to stretch your legs before we head out."

"After I put one of your special handmade diapers on Josiah. Untie me please."

He untied the wrap and laid it on his backpack. She opened the blanket and exposed the infant's naked body. Tiny hands grasped at the air. She slid the small diaper underneath, folded it around the front, and tied the sides. The fabric swallowed his little body but would work until they were back in civilization.

"Perfect. Now you've invented emergency diapers in the wild."

He'd given her some momentary joy before facing a rough day.

She swaddled Josiah, stood and straightened her back.

"Are you ready for another trek through the woods?"

She inhaled and blew out a long breath. "My sore body says it hurts to move. The scrapes on my hands and back sting and ache." She pulled up her shirt sleeves, exposing bruises across her arms. "Not sure which hurt more. The fall or giving birth. I'm as ready as I can be." She turned and faced the waterfall. "I've gotten used to the roar."

Trent analyzed her while she had her back to him. Was he wrong to move her so soon after giving birth? His EMT instructor said women should get up and walk around right after delivery. It could help the healing process go faster and decrease the risk of blood clots. However, he didn't say she should go mountain climbing and starve. At least she had fish for dinner last night.

He'd watch her body language and take it slow. Her ponytail tossed with the breeze. She'd been through a horrific ordeal, and yet she still held up under pressure. He admired her mostly positive attitude and courage.

Rex trotted along the river's edge, stopping occasionally for a drink. His ears perked up, and he held his tail and head high, then proceeded to sniff the ground.

Trent poured the last of the cooled boiled water from the coffeepot into another empty bottle. They had four full bottles of water. He blew out a breath. That should get them through the day. Brooke sat on a boulder, holding Josiah and watching Rex roam. He grabbed his cell and snapped a picture of the picturesque moment. She was stunning. He bit his lip and studied her. Was he ready for an instant family?

She turned back and caught him staring. "You look deep in thought. Anything you want to share?"

He definitely wasn't ready to share the question that came into his mind. "Thinking about the route we should take."

"Do we have a choice?"

He rubbed his forehead. "Since we dropped several feet from the trail, the shortest route is still over the mountain, but it's also the hardest. Altitude could be a problem. Rather than climbing back up to Redbud Trail, I think the easier route, terrain wise, is around the mountain. But it's also longer and more susceptible to wild hog encounters. We'd be a distance from the main trail, which could make it harder for search and rescue."

She took in a breath, and opened her mouth, but clamped it shut. Josiah whimpered. She patted his back and swayed with him.

"Are you asking me to choose?" She moved closer.

"Not necessarily. But time is of the essence." He drew in the sand with a stick. "If we go this way, through the forest, we'd be making our own path until we run into another trail. If we go this way, straight up, the cell tower will be accessible sooner, but you could experience altitude sickness and we could run into your pursuers."

She closed her eyes and rubbed her forehead. "Wild hogs or killers with guns." She dropped her hand from her face. "Cell tower or the probability of another night in the woods. Risk altitude sickness or traipse through unexplored territory." Her eyes bored into his. "Would Josiah have problems breathing in the high altitude? I've already experienced headaches."

"When you put it like that, we don't have a choice. No need to create any more problems than what we already have." He tossed the stick aside. "Around, it is, but we'll still be climbing."

He stood and popped his neck. He wasn't about to risk the high altitude with a newborn. Going around could help, but not totally avoid high terrain. His ankle ached, but not as bad as earlier. A hot shower crossed his mind. His scruffy beard itched.

He picked up the remaining firewood. "Gonna toss these back in the woods and clean up the area." He walked along the river's edge until he'd rounded the curve and tossed the limbs on the ground. The trail up on the ridge was hidden by all the trees.

Rex ran and met him when he returned. Tail wagging and tongue hanging out. Brooke sat on a log near the bank, holding Josiah.

"Did you miss me?" Rex trotted beside him, constantly looking up at him. "Yeah, you did. I can tell. We'll be leaving this scenic place in a few minutes. You can help me protect our guests today."

Rex talked back with a howl and a bark.

He grabbed the coffeepot, scooped water from the river and poured it over the fire, then kicked dirt on top.

No chance of catching the forest on fire, even though only dirt and rocks surrounded them.

"You holding up, okay?"

"Better than I expected. It's eerie out here by myself."

"You get used to it after a while." He sat and dug into the backpack for their morning snacks.

"I suppose, under the right conditions." Skeptical, but she didn't argue.

She sat on a rock across from him. He couldn't help admiring the loose strands of brown hair framing her face and remembering how the reflection of last night's fire danced in her eyes. He scraped a hand over his beard. Normally, he didn't care what he looked like while out camping, but things were different this time. He regretted not having his razor.

"I'll finish the peanut butter crackers from yesterday."

He dug them from the backpack. "Here's your leftover water. We've got more now if you need it. Guess I'll finish the beef jerky I pocketed."

"This is good enough for me." She grew solemn. "Honestly, I'm dreading the journey today."

A howl roared through the camp. She stiffened. "That sounded close. Was it a coyote? Do they run in packs?"

"Coyotes live in family groups, but word has it they usually travel and hunt alone. Attacks on humans are rare. No need to worry."

"So you say."

Chapter Ten

Brooke held Josiah close as she prepared for the hike. Her newfound protective nature kept him warm and shielded him from the fine mist drifting from the waterfall. His every move had her on high alert, and his little squeaks and cries took on new meanings. Hungry. Wet. Stretching. Snuggling. Who knew she'd become so attuned to his needs so quickly?

Light filtered through the trees. A coyote had made its presence known, and she faced another long day. The start of her third day in the wilderness much later than when she'd told her mom she'd be back home. She ached for the mental torture her parents suffered over her disappearance.

She'd made the trip alone. A mistake she'd never live down. Or was it? Would the men have killed whoever joined her? If they'd shoot Nick in cold blood and shoot at Trent, they'd certainly wipe out anyone in the house, except her, until Josiah was born. A chill raced over her body.

Rex reclined at Trent's feet while he finished eating his beef jerky. He was a remarkable man, like none she'd ever met. Could she fall in love so soon after her ex-husband's death? Were her feelings justifiable, or was she merely vulnerable to this brave and compassionate K-9 handler who saved her, delivered Josiah and put his life at risk for them? Her sentiments for him felt right, but she wouldn't know for sure until she was back home in her natural environment. He'd only kissed her. He hadn't said anything about continuing a relationship after they were rescued. He'd only commented about working twenty-four-seven. Not the life she wanted.

She pushed to her feet, holding Josiah. Her legs wobbled and her body rebelled, but she had to move around. Maybe walking today would do her good, although lying back down sounded better.

Rex stood and wagged his tail. A whine escaped. She caught Trent's gaze as Rex allowed her to pat his head. He sniffed her legs. Trent worked with another piece of fabric. "What clever creations are you making now?"

He held up a flat piece of fabric with two slits cut about four inches apart. It's a shirt for Josiah. What do you think?"

Rex walked beside her with his nose in the air, sniffing her baby.

"Rex. Sit." His dog obeyed and sat by his side with his back straight and ears up.

"Perfect design for an infant born in the mountains. I'm impressed."

"Seemed logical your little man needed something around his chest besides the blanket." He handed the creation to her and petted Rex.

She sat on the log and unwrapped her living doll.

His little hands grasped at the air as she slid his arms through the openings and overlapped the extra fabric across his chest. "Fits perfectly."

She lifted Josiah and Trent snapped a photo of him dressed in his matching diaper and shirt. It wasn't the soft onesie from home but would do for now. She quickly swaddled him in the blanket and held him close.

"I could use another drink of water." Had dehydration caught up with her? Weakness coiled itself around her. She guzzled more water than she'd intended, but her body longed for the extra fluid. She capped the bottle and handed it back to Trent.

He pushed it back at her and handed her a small package of trail mix. "Drink all you want. Your body needs it after all you've been through."

She took the trail mix but refused the water, knowing he'd do without to make sure she had what she needed. Wasn't right for him to give up so much when she was the one who'd caused all his problems and put him in this position.

"I'm good for now." Her taste buds tingled at the thought of a latte and a hot cinnamon roll. "What's next?"

"The sooner we get moving, the better." Trent stood and dropped his phone in the outside pocket of his backpack. "If help hasn't arrived by this afternoon, I'll build us a suitable shelter."

"I'm counting on being in my bed tonight. How can I help pack up?"

"Put the propane, cup, Rex's water bowl and whatever else you see in the backpack. I'm going to dispose of this tent."

Rex hopped up and ran to the river, lapping the cold water. He sniffed the ground, the air, and drank more before traipsing off to explore. He returned and followed Trent around.

"Would you put the baby wrap around me, so I don't have to lay him on the ground?"

Trent's face lit up. He retrieved the wrap and tied it snug around her body and neck. Josiah rested against her chest and slept. She gathered all the supplies and arranged them in the bag, noting how low they were on food. At least they had fish last night and still had four bottles of water.

Trent tossed the supporting limbs from their make-do shelter.

"Are we taking it with us?"

"Part of it." He pulled out his pocketknife and cut one whole sidewall out of the rough fabric, folded the thickness, and stuffed it into his bulging backpack. He folded his knife and dropped it into his pocket before crumpling the remaining piece in a pile and placing it under the overhang of the tree root where it once stood.

"This will have to do until I can return and discard it properly." He dusted his hands and turned to her. "I know I keep asking this, but are you ready?"

His light green eyes blended with the various shades of green in the forest. He'd proven himself as a man of integrity and he'd won her trust, mostly. She'd called him trustworthy, but she'd know for sure if he got them to safety. How many times had Nick made promises and never followed through? She'd lost count. Her insides churned at the thought of making another wrong decision, like she had with Nick. It felt right trusting Trent, but was she falling into another failed relationship?

She propped her hands at her waist. "What woman who just birthed a baby do you think would be up for this task?" She lifted her eyebrows and waited for an answer.

He rubbed his unshaven chin. "Guess you've got a point." He checked his compass, hooked the leash on Rex and handed her a walking stick. "Made us new ones."

She placed one hand under Josiah's body and gripped the stick. "You're so resourceful." She followed behind him and hobbled over the rocky surface. "Too bad we have to leave the beauty and sound of the waterfall."

"Oh, so you decided it's beautiful. We can come back after all this is over. Uh, I mean, it's always here if you ever want to return."

"I've seen too much already." She grinned at his slipup. At least he didn't act like he resented the trouble she'd caused him.

He stopped and looked around. "No signs of those guys so far. Keep your ears open. They will have reached the top by now. I'm certain they'll head back down to where they lost sight of us. They know we're moving slow and will widen their search."

"There you go again. Casting more fear into my already skeptical thoughts." She huffed. "You're such a guy. I don't need to know the scary parts. All I need is encouraging, positive comments to keep me going." A shot of espresso would boost her energy. Wasn't her favorite beverage, but it might help regain her waning strength, and they'd only just begun the hike. She had no choice but to push forward as much as her body allowed, and then some.

Trent paused at the curve in the river. His chest swelled when he took in a deep breath. Rex stood beside him and seemed to mimic his handler. The man and his canine knew each other well. She'd grown to appreciate their trust in each other.

"Looks like Richard and Dale trekked through this way. It's too far downhill to get back on the main track." He pulled out his compass and glanced back at her. "Need to cross the river and go up the other side."

Her mouth flew open. "Cross the river?" The pounding in her chest increased. No way would she risk falling with her baby.

"It narrows farther down and will be safer." His stare searched her. "We'll cross over and see where it leads us."

"I thought you knew this place." *Breathe, just breathe. He's doing his best.* Uncertainty gripped her gut.

"I've been on several trails in these mountains, but never ventured off Redbud Trail. We're exploring unfamiliar territory."

He led her along the riverbank. He was right. It narrowed into a stream. "I'll go first."

"Don't fall in. Not in my plan today."

Only four steps across the knee-deep, mildly flowing water and he made it to the other side. She followed without any problems, and they discovered a small trail.

Rex's tail stuck out as he sniffed the ground and stared into the wooded terrain. The dog's behavior and the flattened grass convinced her they were following some animal's trail not meant for hiking. Were they headed toward danger? How many extra miles would this path distance them from the ranger's station? Could she even make it that far?

Trent pushed up the steep incline, with Rex leading the way. Doubts of making the right decision ate at him. His stomach churned. If he stayed due north, they should be fine, but this menial path proved tougher than the Redbud. He glanced back at Brooke. Risks went with whichever decision they made. Would they have been better off to take their chances with the killers on the loose? Maybe. Change in the altitude could cause problems.

Her knuckles whitened as she gripped her stick with one hand and patted Josiah with the other. How much longer would she last? He scolded himself for taking them off course. Had he gotten them lost? Were they going the right direction? His compass said go this way. Must be right. Hunger ripped at his gut and the lack of water was getting the best of him. He paused and took a big swallow.

She trudged along behind him, moving in slow motion. If she could muster up the strength to move faster, maybe they'd hit a better trail and find help.

"I know it's hard on you, but the faster we move, the sooner we'll find help."

"Now *that's* encouraging," she said.

Good thing she didn't know there were wild pigs in this area. Not to mention the usual bears, mountain lions, coyotes and all the other wildlife. If she thought about it, she wouldn't let too much distance come between them.

"Do you need my hand?" Of course, she did. Why ask? His stomach growled again.

"No. I can do this myself."

She held the walking stick with both hands, placed it in front of her, and visibly trudged forward. Josiah hung against her body in the wrap he'd made.

Rex walked into the edge of the tall grass with his ears perked at high alert. Trent scanned the forest while waiting for Brooke to catch up. He spotted a blackberry vine. "Hey, I found us some berries."

He traipsed off the path, pulling the empty water bottle from the loop on his belt. He filled it with the globe-shaped berries, blew on a couple and popped them into his mouth. The splash of sweet flavor tickled his taste buds.

Brooke leaned against a boulder. "I'll wait here. Saving my steps."

He popped several more in his mouth before returning to the trail. "Here, eat these. The sugar will help with energy and they're full of vitamin C and antioxidants."

"Are they safe?" She held it up and inspected it.

He dropped his shoulders and stared at her. "I wouldn't give you anything that would hurt you. Just because you're not in a grocery store doesn't mean they aren't good. There are plenty of berries that aren't edible. You just have to study and be able to recognize them. Blow on it to make sure there are no ants or bugs, then eat it."

She threw it down. "I'm not taking a chance of eating bugs."

"I promise you the berries are safe."

A loud, long puff of breath sounded with each berry she blew on. He'd gotten his fill and felt more refreshed. She downed several, kissed Josiah on the head and patted his back.

"Need to refill the bottle for later." He took off through the tall grass with Rex at his heels and stuffed more of the tasty treats into the bottle. A rustle in the woods caught his attention. His heart jumped into his throat. Berries were a bear's dining table. He should have thought about that before they lingered too long. He rushed back to the path. "Come on. Got to get moving. I heard something. We aren't the only ones who love the sweet taste of berries."

"Don't scare me." She grabbed her stick and followed him. "I can't move as fast as you."

"Do the best you can. Come on." He turned and high-stepped upward. He'd grown weary with little to no sleep, and he couldn't decide if his kiss meant anything to her. Relationship or not, she needed to keep up with him. Getting back to his job didn't sound so bad.

An exasperated gasp filled his ears as they trekked up the mountain. After they were a safe distance away, Trent glanced back. A big buck stood on the path below them. Trent's shoulders relaxed and his eyes fell on Brooke. Her head was down, still gripping the stick until she caught up with him. She stopped and looked up at him. Tears rolled down her cheeks.

His breath caught. Her big blue eyes glistened through the wetness, and her red face told him he'd pushed her too hard. He reached out and pulled her close.

"Let's find a place to rest. You're doing great."

Her lip quivered as she wiped her cheeks. "I'm tired and my body aches. I told you I can't move fast. And I need to feed Josiah again. My husband is dead. I can't call anyone, and I've ruined your camping trip. Leaning on you for everything is difficult for me. I don't want to move another inch, but my life and the life of my baby depend on it. Do you call all that doing great?"

He cleared his throat. "I know this is a lot. But try looking at the bright side. You're alive. Josiah is warm and safe. We haven't starved or been attacked by bears, and we've avoided the killers. If I could carry you, I would." He dropped his arm from around her shoulders and helped her sit on a tree stump. "I'll keep watch while you feed Josiah and take a break."

Rex pivoted and stared up in the trees, growling.

"What is it, boy?" The hum of a bullet whizzed past his ear and hit a tree. Too close. He grabbed Brooke and fell behind a rock. Bullets chipped the stone and bounced off. Rex danced on the leash, baring his teeth, barking, and growling. Trent reeled him in. "Quiet. Good eye."

"They found us." Fear spilled through Brooke's voice. Josiah whimpered, and she consoled him as best she could under the circumstances.

"Not sure where they are." He squinted and peered through the trees until he spotted them up on the ridge. "They're at a higher elevation overlooking the valley. My guess is they are still on Redbud Trail, a distance away, but yes, we're on their radar."

Another shot pinged the rock above Trent's head.

"They're shooting at you." Her breathing edged in hyperventilation. "What are we going to do?"

"First, you're going to focus on breathing normally." He kissed her forehead. "It's okay. You'll be fine. They figure if they can get rid of me, you'll be an easy catch. Right now, they're up on the ridge, too far away to rush in after us. Let's stay close to these boulders and crawl until we reach the dense forest. We'll figure out what to do from there."

"Crawl?" She groaned. "You're putting me through a crash survival course and testing my endurance, aren't you?"

"You said it, not me. If only it were a test. It's easier learning without the death threat, though." He touched her back. "Did I hurt you or Josiah when I jerked you down?"

"No. I'm mad at myself for being emotional and crying like a baby. It's not like me to feel sorry for myself, and here you are, the target of their wrath. You seem to hold up just fine under pressure. If anything happens to you, I'll never forgive myself."

"Nothing's going to happen to me, and you *do* have extenuating circumstances that could cause a smorgasbord of emotions." He couldn't imagine going through all the trauma she'd encountered the past two days. She deserved a medal for bravery.

"Still, I'll focus on doing better, and you have to stay alive." She patted Josiah and kissed his head. He squirmed and let out a squeaky cry. "Not now, little guy, not now."

"I'm not going anywhere. If it helps any, I think

you're an extraordinarily brave lady after all you've endured. I admire your determination and the way you've faced your fears of the wild." She'd forced him to face his self-doubts and fears, and for that, he was grateful.

"You're just being nice. I'm still scared stiff."

"Rightfully so." He checked his compass again. "Guess we better keep moving. Follow me."

He kept Rex close to his side as they crawled along the base of the rocks. Spiders raced up the stone, black ants scattered and a few ladybugs crawled across blades of grass. If she spotted them, she might hop to her feet and scream. He'd best keep her focused on the thicket ahead.

"See that group of pine trees? Concentrate on them. We'll be out of the killer's shooting range once we get there."

"My friends will never believe I hiked, had a baby and crawled on all fours in the woods. I don't believe it myself."

The shade of the pine trees confirmed their closeness to safety. Trent hopped up and helped Brooke to her feet. Josiah's whimpers escalated into full-blown cries. His arms escaped the wrap and his hands opened and closed.

"He's hungry and probably wet. Can you untie the wrap and let me change and feed him?" She turned so fast her ponytail slapped him across the face. He brushed the hair away and smiled. She could do that any day.

"While you take care of Josiah, I'm going to scout around and get a take on our position." Rex took advantage of the lengthened leash, sniffing the ground, the base of trees, and marking his territory.

She grabbed his arm. "Don't leave me here by myself."

Chapter Eleven

The idea of being alone even for a minute in the middle of nowhere made Brooke's insides knot up and twist. *I'm not a wimp even though I've argued, cried and whined.* She reasoned that the only real danger she'd faced wasn't the bears she'd feared for so long. It was being captured by those killers.

She gazed down at the miniature human she'd birthed. His little fingers tightened in a fist and pressed against his cheeks as she fed him. His wispy blond hair lay curled against his scalp. She cupped his small, fragile head with her hand and held him close until he finished eating. After a burp and a diaper change, he went back to sleep. If she were home, she'd sit for hours, rocking and admiring him. If only.

Rex ran to her and licked Josiah's head. His tail wagged, and his dark eyes kept a keen watch. He ran back to Trent, who leaned against the opposite side of one of the pine trees nearby.

Her cheeks warmed. "You can come back now. Thanks for respecting my privacy.

"You're welcome. Hold still so I can snap a couple of memorable photos." His green eyes brightened with his smile.

He pushed away from the tree and walked toward her, holding the baby wrap. His long legs, masculine build, and good looks weakened her in ways she hadn't felt in years. His protective nature and survival skills assured her he'd do whatever it took to get them to safety.

"Guess that means you're ready to keep moving." She drew in a deep breath, exhaled and stood so he could tie the wrap. "Did you find anything?"

"After we pass through these pine trees, we'll face another incline."

"I thought we were taking the easy way around." She stared at him.

"There's nothing easy about hiking, whether up or around. Even going around, we still climb upward only at a more tolerable ascent."

"Any sign of those guys?"

"Nope." He rubbed his eyes, then looked at her. "They may have…"

Rex growled and rushed toward the depths of the pines as far as his leash allowed. A grunting, squealing sound met with Trent's ears. He tugged on the leash. "Rex. Come."

Rex returned with his ears laid back, his fur raised on his spine, and tail straight. He continued growling, looked to Trent, then back into the forest.

"What is it? A wild hog?" Fear emanated in her voice.

"Yep. I could shoot it, but the shot would give our

location away. We need to get moving. Those things are destructive and dangerous."

His jaw tightened. He gripped her hand firmly. Adrenaline rushed over her and pushed her weak body forward like a bungee cord. No doubts, she'd collapse once they were out of danger.

Rex danced on the leash, fighting to get to the animal. He looked like he'd rip the creature to shreds if Trent would let him loose.

"Quiet, Rex."

Rex obeyed. He kept the length of the leash tight. If she read him right, he wanted to fight and protect them.

The squealing and snorting grew closer. Her foot caught on a tree root and she stumbled forward. Trent caught her before she fell face-first on top of Josiah.

"I can't keep this pace." She blinked back threatening tears. Her emotions were all over the place today. Just the thought of her unstable feelings made her want to cry.

"We'll slow down before one of us gets hurt. If I have to shoot it, I will, but running isn't worth the risk." He wrapped his arm around her shoulders. "Can you keep walking?"

"Not much choice, is there?" She leaned on him for added strength. Walking was one thing but running up a mountain wasn't in her recovery orders.

They emerged from the pine trees into an open field. The squealing faded, and she released the breath she'd held. The sun rose higher, but the temperatures remained cool. Her head spun for a moment and stopped.

"My head spins now and then." She pressed her hand against her forehead. "And I'm getting a headache."

"You're exhausted, dehydrated and half starved. We're still climbing and getting into higher altitudes. Not as high as the trail, though."

She struggled with each breath. Carrying extra weight hadn't changed much. Inside or out, she still had Josiah with her.

"If you could go anywhere in the world, where would you go?" he asked.

She had a feeling he was trying to distract her from the danger surrounding them. "Someday, I'd like to go to Alaska to hike with all those grizzlies."

He glanced back. "Oh, you know about the grizzlies?"

"I do watch nature shows. I'm not totally ignorant."

"I think you must be pretty knowledgeable to own your own business." He hefted himself up on a rock that blocked their path and offered his hand.

She welcomed the help and stepped up beside him. "Evidently, I'm not as smart as I thought. I'm wondering if Nick lost my business in his shenanigans. His name was on the deed, too. Guess I'll find out when I get home and check the damages to our finances."

"What will you do after you get home, besides bury your husband, care for Josiah and monitor your business?"

"Get back in church and get on with my life. What about you?"

"Hmm, living alone isn't all it's made out to be. Think I'll get back in the dating scene and see what God has planned. I even considered asking you out."

"But what about your demanding job? I thought it consumed your time?"

"It does if I allow it."

Her heart pounded in her ears. Each step up the wooded trail a chore. Had she heard him right? She'd ponder the idea. Dreams of home, a nice shower, clean clothes, a hot meal and her own bed danced in her head, that was, after being released from the hospital. *Focus. One foot in front of the other.*

"So where would you go if you could go anywhere? Back to the mountains?" She rolled her eyes and expected a camping response.

"Italy or England. Traveling abroad has always interested me."

"That's shocking. I assumed you'd return to the forest."

"I live close enough to the mountains that I can visit whenever I want. Exploring new territories overseas sounds intriguing."

"I've always wanted to go to Italy. Maybe some… ouch, ouch, ouch!" She danced in place, slapping at her leg.

Rex backed away, barking.

Trent spun. "What's wrong?"

"Something bit me." She slapped as her leg.

"Fire ants." He brushed the ants off her leg. You must have stepped on a fire ant mound. An army of them will crawl up and all sting at one time. It's going to hurt and make red welts around your ankle, then it will start itching or burning. Let's find a place to stop. I've got hydrocortisone cream in my first aid kit."

She slapped at her leg again and stomped her feet. Heat rose to her face. "Are they still on me? Will they attack Josiah?" She shivered. "How am I supposed to see the ground with all these overgrown weeds? Why aren't you bothered by any of this stuff? Why am I always the one causing problems?"

He sat her on a stump. She jumped to her feet and searched the ground and around the stump. "Is it safe? Is something else going to bite me?" She lost her balance and her breathing increased. "I... I can't breathe."

Rex drew closer and stood, watching her.

"Sit down. You're hyperventilating. Don't want you to pass out." He rambled through his bag and pulled out a small paper bag. "Here, hold this over your mouth and focus on breathing slow and steady for a few breaths. Six to twelve is recommended."

He untied the baby wrap.

"Giving you a break." He lifted Josiah into his arms. "We're good. Breathe. Focus. Relax."

"My heart is racing. Is it the altitude?" Concern edged in a panic attack. Would she die up here?

Trent held her baby in one arm like a football while he applied the medication on the bites with a small gauze pad. Her leg burned. Felt like two armies of ants zeroed in on her one leg. The itching intensified. She had to scratch it. He moved her hand away.

"It's going to burn and itch for about ten minutes. Give it time to calm down. Keep your hands off." He pointed to the bag. "Use the bag again. Controlled breathing is what you need. Breathe in slowly through your nose. Then, gradually blow out through your mouth. Focus on that pattern until you feel you're in control again."

She complied. Every vein in her body throbbed.

He stood in front of her, patting Josiah on the back.

Kiera guessed an hour at least had passed, possibly two, when they suddenly heard a door slam shut.

"Where are they going?" she whispered. Even as she spoke, she realized only one of them might have gone outside. The other could still be in the cabin.

"I don't know."

"Do you think they'll leave?"

"I'm praying they do. We just have to wait."

In the hidden confines of the cubby, Kiera pictured her and Nash coming out of this alive. Marshal Gifford and the operative wouldn't remain here forever. They'd eventually give up or leave for fear of getting caught. Then Kiera, Heather and Nash would go for help on the snowmobile.

"Kiera?"

"Yes?" She smoothed her hand over Heather's hair.

"When this is over," he said, "I want to see you again."

"Oh, Nash." Definitely not what she'd been expecting him to say. "My life is a mess. I'm in witness protection. I can't just *see* a guy."

"I know. Humor me, okay? I need something positive to hold on to right now. The thought that we could be sitting across from each other having dinner one day. It's another reason to fight like crazy and not quit."

"I would really like that. And I'm not just humoring you."

He reached for her hand and brought it to his cheek. "God has a plan for us. Something good. I can feel it."

"I want to believe that, too."

He linked their fingers. "I care about you. I wanted you to know that."

She heard what he didn't say. *In case we don't survive.*

"I care about you, too."

"I think I'd make a great dad."

"You would. You will."

Kiera's eyes filled with tears. She wiped them away and leaned into Nash. Their world shrank to the small dark space where they hid. For a brief reprise, there was only the three of them, connected physically, emotionally and spiritually. Heather's regular breathing marked the passing minutes. Kiera began to hope Marshal Gifford and the operative were truly gone for good.

A thought occurred to her. Or, more accurately, she remembered something. "Law enforcement must be looking for me. The US Marshals' office would have alerted them when we didn't arrive in Flagstaff."

"True. And Gifford's car is on the main road. County workers will be out first thing this morning, checking on people and any damage now that it's stopped snowing. They'll call in an abandoned vehicle, especially one that's crashed into a tree. Though, no one would know to look for you here."

"But there's a chance. It's something."

"It's something," he agreed.

And as the moments continued to pass, Kiera's optimism grew.

It evaporated when they heard the unmistakable sound of footsteps in the bedroom. The sound stopped right outside the cubby door. Six feet away.

Nash reached beneath his coat and felt for the fishing knife at his waist. The only thing they had in their favor was the element of surprise. Gifford knew he and Kiera had knives, but the operative didn't. If the right moment presented itself, Nash could use the knife to disable the man.

Right. And pigs could fly.

But hadn't David defeated the giant, Goliath, with just a sling and a stone?

The footsteps moved around the bedroom, receding, stopping outside the cubby door and receding again.

Nash wanted to believe the operative and Gifford were preparing to leave or removing DNA evidence. Much more likely, the operative had contacted his superiors with his satellite phone and received an update on when his reinforcements would arrive—which would probably be any minute.

And, if Nash's prayers were answered, the operative and his reinforcements would head into the woods on whatever vehicle he'd arrived on, allowing Nash, Kiera and Heather to escape with the snowmobile. If Gifford remained behind, Nash was confident he could overtake her. Or convince her to let them go.

Eventually, whoever was in the bedroom left and went downstairs. Nash and Kiera breathed a little easier. But they were far from safe.

At certain times, Gifford and the operative made a ruckus. Other times, the cabin was unnervingly quiet. Whenever they came upstairs, Nash's blood rushed through his veins like a raging river. Kiera would utter small scared sounds and inch nearer to him. Not that it did any good, but he wondered why the operative and Gifford hadn't stayed out longer searching for them. They might have become wise to Nash's ruse and weren't waiting for reinforcements at all. Except the operative had bragged about that fact earlier. If only

Nash had X-ray vision and could see through walls and floors.

Suddenly, the footsteps returned and were right outside the cubby. Or by the window? Did they notice the jimmied lock? It was impossible to tell. Beside him, Kiera curled into a protective ball around Heather and scooted farther behind the crate.

Nash shifted. He inched himself in front of her as much as possible. The waiting and not knowing was excruciating. Anticipation gnawed at him with sharp teeth.

He put his hand on her knee.

Her response was a strangled sob.

Heather whined.

"Hush, baby." Kiera's teeth chattered.

A thud in the bedroom had her gasping and digging her nails into Nash's arms. Gifford's muffled voice reached them in the back of the cubby. Nash couldn't make out her words. Eventually, silence descended again. He sensed Kiera's lips moving and heard a hushed word here and there. She was praying.

He joined her until questions invaded his thoughts. How soon until dawn? Would the county begin plowing the roads right away or wait? His parents would be on their way here before long. He didn't want to consider the possibility of them arriving while the operative and Gifford were still here. Or, worse, discover dead bodies, one of them their son's.

Thundering footsteps on the stairs emptied his brain of everything except fear and dread and the instinct to save himself, Kiera and Heather. He barely had a chance to determine where Gifford and the operative were when the footsteps came straight to the cubby door. No doubt about their exact location this time.

Kiera shuddered and pushed Heather to the floor. Nash ducked below the crate.

"I've got you," he repeated his earlier promise and hoped he could keep it.

"Show me!" the operative's voice penetrated the cubby door.

His demand was accompanied by a loud thump that could only be the straight back chair sitting outside the door being hurled across the room.

Nash fought to remain in control. He couldn't fall apart. Not now, or they were doomed. His worst nightmare became a reality when the cubby door flew open and a flashlight beam sliced the darkness.

"Found you," the operative said as the beam danced over the crate. "Aren't you clever."

Kiera screamed and covered her face with her arm. Nash tried to shield her, but his efforts were in vain. They'd been discovered, and there was no other way out of the cubby.

"Good job, Marshal," the operative said. "You figured out where they went. Earned your paycheck for the week."

"No, no, no," Kiera cried and scrambled backward. Only she had nowhere to go. They were surrounded by solid walls on three sides. "Leave us alone."

"Are they unharmed?" Gifford asked.

The operative snorted. "For the moment. Ask me again in an hour." Then he growled, "Get out."

"No," Kiera cried again.

"Have it your way. I'll shoot you now. Makes no difference to me."

Nash believed him. Cruelty lay beneath the operative's humorous tone. He no longer cared about being caught or their deaths looking like an accident. They'd outsmarted him, and he wasn't happy about it.

"Kiera," Nash coaxed. "Do as he says."

She shook her head. Tears spilled from her eyes, and she crushed Heather in a fierce hug. "I can't. I won't."

"We have to. Remember," he added in a low voice, "as long as we're alive, we have a chance." Minuscule though it was. "I'll go first." Pushing the crate aside, Nash got to his knees and crawled forward.

"That's right," the operative said, pleased with himself.

Halfway to the door, Nash awkwardly pivoted in the cramped space and faced Kiera. "Hon. We need to go."

"Now." The operative was done toying with them.

"Kiera." Nash reached out a hand to her. "Don't give him a reason to shoot."

She reluctantly took his hand, drawing on the courage at her core, and let him lead her to the cubby door.

The moment Nash backed into the room, a gun was shoved into the base of his skull.

"Get up, you pathetic piece of garbage."

He released Kiera's hand, sucked in a breath and climbed slowly to his feet, acutely aware of the cold gun barrel digging into his flesh. Before he was fully standing, the operative hooked him by the arm and thrust him aside.

"Keep your gun on him," the operative instructed Gifford.

She leveled her Glock at Nash, and he noted the rope burns at her wrists. A nervous tic caused her left eye to twitch. That and the sweat beading on her brow, gave Nash an uneasy feeling. She was a time bomb ready to explode.

The operative reached into the cubby and pulled Kiera out, his long fingers gripping her arm like steel claws. She resisted, Heather tucked close to her chest, and tried to break free.

The operative jammed his gun into her side. "Knock it off."

Nash took a step in their direction.

"Stay where you are," Gifford ordered.

He obeyed. Her nervous tic could travel to her trigger finger.

"Get your hands off me," Kiera demanded in a harsh voice.

"With pleasure." He pushed her toward Nash. She almost lost her balance before Nash caught her.

"Whatever you do with us," he said, righting Kiera, "leave the baby here for someone to find."

"Shut your mouth," the operative snapped and hitched his chin toward the bedroom door. "Now, downstairs. Time's wasting."

Nash put his arm around Kiera's shoulders.

She raised desperate eyes to his. Her entire body shook. "He's going to kill my baby."

Heather opened her mouth and howled.

The operative's expression turned vicious. "Do something about that brat or I will."

"Please, no." Kiera went weak in the knees.

"Stay with me," Nash said, supporting her. "We'll get our chance."

His words seemed to give her strength.

The operative closed the distance between them. "That's it. I've had enough."

"No," Gifford said. "If you kill them here, the murders will be traced to me and the 7-Crowns. Your superiors were specific. Nothing to connect them."

"I'm sick of your nagging."

"Stick to the plan." Her eye tic worsened, but she remained resolute.

Nash harbored no illusions that she was helping them. She was protecting herself and her own children.

Fuming, the operative stepped behind Nash and jammed the gun barrel between his shoulder blades. He then propelled Nash and Kiera toward the door. They stumbled but kept going.

In the hallway, at the top of the stairs, Kiera abruptly spun around. "Marshal Gifford. You can't let him kill us."

"It'll go easier for you if you don't resist."

"May God forgive you."

"I've made my choice," Gifford said. "I'll deal with the consequences."

"I'm sick of all this bellyaching." The operative gave Kiera a shove.

Nash grabbed her before she toppled down the stairs. With his other hand, he gripped the bannister, steadying them both. Each step they took brought them closer to their deaths.

At the bottom of the stairs, he saw the clock on the fireplace mantel. Three-forty in the morning. The operative had more than enough time before daylight to take them into the woods and dispose of them. But how did he intend to transport them? The snow was too deep for a truck, even one with all-wheel drive.

"Which way?" Nash asked at the bottom of the stairs.

"Don't be an idiot." The operative pushed Nash and Kiera in the direction of the kitchen.

Kiera tripped and cried out. Heather's constant crying was punctuated by hiccups.

Nash caught a glimpse of Gifford behind the operative. Every trace of the confidence she'd exhibited when he'd first encountered her had fled. She appeared as scared as they were. Maybe she feared she'd be murdered in the woods, too. A loose end tied up.

In the kitchen, Kiera's frightened glance connected with his. He wanted to assure her they'd be all right. The best he could do was send a silent message that he would stay with her till the end if necessary and not let them be separated. She seemed to understand and take a small measure of comfort from that.

The operative propelled Nash and Kiera to the mudroom. "Get dressed like normal people and not some homeless bums."

Kiera shook her head mutely.

"Don't make me repeat myself."

"He wants us to wear our parkas and gloves and ski pants," Nash said. "So it doesn't look suspicious when our bodies are found."

The operative sneered at him. "Give the guy a gold star."

Kiera didn't move.

"Get her to cooperate," he said to Nash, "Or I'll put

her in the clothes. And I assure you, she won't like it. You have to the count of three."

"Don't refuse him, Kiera," Nash said.

"Heather's snowsuit is upstairs," she answered softly.

"Give me a break." The operative shoved Nash aside and trained the gun on Heather. "Maybe I'll get rid of the brat now and dump her body down the well."

Kiera screamed and twisted sideways, her arms going protectively around Heather.

Nash didn't stop to consider his actions. He stepped in front of Kiera, directly into the line of fire.

Chapter Twelve

Kiera dropped to her knees behind Nash, closed her eyes and used her body to shield Heather.

Lord, take me. Spare my baby.

She waited for the gunshot. And waited. It didn't come.

A series of sickening thuds, followed by a low grunt, dared her to sneak a peek. She let out a sharp gasp. Nash stood doubled over and clutching his middle, his breathing ragged. A bruise on his left cheek grew brighter and angrier by the second. The operative nursed his right hand.

"Do us both a favor," he snarled at Nash with hatred and anger. "Don't try to be a hero again."

Kiera wanted to go to Nash and check on him. She didn't dare move.

With visible effort, he straightened and shook his head as if to clear it. Kiera fretted. He must be hurting. That didn't stop him from glaring at the operative. She feared for his safety. He was going to get himself killed if he went too far.

"Marshal. Help us, please," she begged.

The other woman considered a moment before saying to the operative, "Let me get the kid a snowsuit. What's the harm?"

A snowsuit? Kiera had been hoping for more.

"I don't think so," the operative said.

"I won't be long."

"You have a real problem with following orders, don't you?"

They stood facing each other for several seconds. The marshal broke eye contact first. As she lowered her gaze, she raised her Glock.

"Wrong move, lady." The operative redirected his gun away from Nash and toward her.

"Hey. What are you doing?" she demanded. "I wasn't going to—" She retreated a step. "You're making a mistake."

"Afraid you've become a liability."

He took aim. The marshal's cheeks drained of color. Kiera suppressed a scream and covered Heather's eyes. Her baby shouldn't see this.

"Think about what you're doing," the marshal said, her voice faltering.

"I have."

Kiera alone noticed Nash carefully reaching beneath his coat. His fingers emerged with the fishing knife he'd been carrying.

"I'm through thinking," the operative said. "I prefer action."

Lowering his head, Nash charged, the knife extended. He slammed into the operative. Caught off guard, the man stumbled, his hand going to the wound at his side. His eyes widened, more with surprise than pain. Nash pressed his advantage, and the two of them toppled to the floor, struggling for control of the gun. The operative fought back, surprisingly strong for having been stabbed in the side. Nash, too, considering his beating.

Terror gripped Kiera around the throat with sharp, icy talons. She retreated partially into the pantry. She had to protect Heather.

"Do something," she yelled to the marshal, to God, to anyone who would listen.

Heather cried and flailed her arms and legs.

Kiera bit back a sob and shrieked in alarm when a gun went off. The marshal's, not the operative's. She stood in the center of the kitchen, her legs braced and her Glock raised.

Kiera watched and waited for the patch of telltale blood to appear on the operative's shirt or head. It didn't. She looked closer. No evidence of a wound. And he continued to fight Nash with the strength of a grizzly.

What had happened?

And then, Kiera saw a circle of blood appear in the middle of Nash's thigh. No! It couldn't be. The marshal had hit Nash instead of the operative. But she was supposed to be an expert marksman.

"You shot him," Kiera accused.

The marshal's eye twitched frantically. "I meant to shoot the operative."

Kiera forced her gaze back to the two men locked in hand-to-hand combat on the kitchen floor. She was horrified to see the operative had Nash pinned beneath him.

He brought his gun to Nash's temple. Nash grabbed

the operative's wrist and tried to push the gun away. He failed. The operative's hand refused to budge. In another second, he'd shoot Nash, and the marshal was no help whatsoever.

Kiera's feet moved with a will of their own. They carried her to where the two men struggled. She stared at them, at Nash, who fought with incredible courage. He didn't deserve this. All he'd ever done was try to help her. Treat her kindly. Care for her. For that and more, he'd pay with his life.

"Stop right now." The voice coming from the marshal sounded inhuman. The hand leveling her weapon at the two men trembled. "Or I'll shoot."

No one seemed to hear her or care. With a fist like a wrecking ball, the operative punched Nash in the face, leaving him in a daze. He half turned and, without missing a beat, fired his gun at the marshal. She flew backward, off her feet and into the kitchen table, and then crashed to the floor where she lay unmoving, her eyes closed.

Kiera gasped. Another murder because of the 7-Crowns Syndicate. Nash would be next. Then Kiera and Heather. It would never stop.

"I'm gonna put you in the well instead of that brat," the operative said to Nash and shoved the gun barrel into the soft flesh beneath his chin.

No, he wasn't. Not if Kiera could help it.

She grabbed the penknife out of her pocket. Protecting Heather with one arm, she bent down and stabbed the operative in his back.

He yelped and jerked.

Somewhere in her mind, Kiera knew the injury

wasn't lethal. Her sole intent had been to prevent him from killing Nash.

Roaring like an enraged animal, the operative pushed off Nash and sprang to his feet, the entire side of his shirt a dark red from the other wound he'd sustained. Kiera jumped in alarm and staggered away from him She wasn't fast enough, and he grabbed for Heather.

Kiera swung the baby away and out of his reach. "Leave her alone!"

The gun appeared in her face. Large. Black. Deadly. She froze, gripping Heather like a vice.

"That little trick will cost you," he threatened.

She shut her eyes and prayed for the end to be swift and that she and Heather wouldn't suffer.

Nash's ragged shout filled the kitchen. "Get away from her."

Kiera's eyes flew open. She stared in disbelief as Nash yanked the operative away from her and Heather. He must have summoned strength from somewhere inside him, for he slammed his fist into the operative's face with the force of a cyclone. The gun sailed out of the operative's hand and landed several feet away.

She ran over and kicked the gun beneath the kitchen table, too afraid to pick it up while she held Heather. She hurried to the marshal and kicked her gun under the table as well.

Nash and the operative continued to struggle, though it now appeared that Nash had the upper hand. He pushed the operative to the counter, bending him backward over it. Using his entire forearm to restrain the operative, Nash grabbed the ceramic cookie jar with his other hand and smashed it twice into the operative's head. The energy drained from him, and he crumpled to the floor as if in slow motion. His eyes closed and he appeared to lose consciousness.

Kiera rushed to Nash.

"Are you okay?"

Chest heaving, he leaned against the counter and pointed. "Get the rope the operative left in the mud-room."

She fetched it. Heather was inconsolable, and Kiera silently promised her daughter she would comfort her soon. First, they needed to incapacitate the operative and get away.

Nash flipped the operative onto his stomach and tied his hands behind his back. He then bound the operative's ankles together, just as the man started to rouse. A large bump already appeared on the side of his head where he'd been struck with the cookie jar.

"You're not going to get away with this," he grumbled thickly. "My people will hunt you down."

"We'll see."

"You're dead. You're all dead."

Nash struggled to his feet, wincing as his did. Blood soaked his jeans. That wound had to hurt like the dickens.

With some effort, he dragged the operative to the pantry where he shut him in and engaged the sliding lock. It wasn't much. The operative, if he weren't tied, could probably break down the door. He still may be able to by ramming it with his shoulder.

As if echoing her thoughts, Nash said, "That won't hold him for long. We need to hurry."

"What about your leg? Can you drive the snowmobile?"

"I'll be fine."

She wasn't sure about that, but since she couldn't drive, they had no other choice.

In the mudroom, she plucked one of Nash's mom's scarves off the hook. "Here. You can use this as a bandage to stop the bleeding."

From inside the pantry came the sounds of movement.

"No time," Nash said.

"Do it," Kiera insisted in a tone that let him know she wasn't going anywhere with him until he applied the makeshift bandage.

He tied the scarf around his thigh. Just as he was knotting it, they heard a quiet groan from the kitchen.

"The marshal! She's alive." Kiera hurried over to where the woman lay.

Kneeling beside her, Kiera set Heather down on the floor. She checked over the marshal, not sure what to look for. Her breathing was shallow and uneven, and her pallor a ghastly white. She didn't move, and her eyes remained closed. Kiera untied the scarf from her neck and pressed it to the marshal's upper chest in an attempt to stem the bleeding there. The wound looked much too close to her heart.

Nash limped over. "Is she conscious?"

"No." Kiera stared up at him. "What should we do? We can't leave her."

"We'll send help."

"She may not live that long."

He scooped up Heather from the floor. "We have to get out of here."

"Marshal Gifford?" Kiera gently prodded the woman's arm.

She didn't respond.

"Kiera. If we stay, we'll die. If we go, we'll live. Heather will live."

"Okay." While Kiera knew he was right, that didn't make leaving the marshal any easier. "We'll send help," she told the unconscious woman. "You hang in there. You hear me? Don't die."

Nash lifted her by the arm and hustled her to the mudroom. There, they added gloves and ski pants to the multilayer of outerwear they still wore. Kiera again stuffed Heather down inside her coats, leaving only the baby's cap-covered head exposed.

Heather instantly calmed in her familiar cocoon.

"Let's go," Nash said.

He and Kiera headed outside by way of the carport. They trudged, Nash with obvious difficulty, through the deep snow to where the operative had left the snow-mobile in the middle of the backyard. He removed the spare key from his coat pocket, and they climbed on.

Hearing a low whine in the distance, Kiera asked, "What's that?"

Nash's answer was a forceful, "No matter what happens, keep your head down."

Nash ignored the fireworks exploding in his injured leg. He inserted the spare key, and the snowmobile's engine churned to life. While Kiera tucked Heather soundly between them, he attached the safety strap to his jacket. Should he fall from the snowmobile, the engine would automatically shut off and prevent a runaway.

There were no seat belts. He'd take any turns carefully while going as fast as he possibly dared. They had no goggles, either, and couldn't spare precious time to locate some in the shed.

"Grab on," he told Kiera.

She reached her arms around his waist and locked her hands together. He felt Heather squirm against his back.

He eased the snowmobile forward. During the night, the operative had followed the false tracks into the woods. Nash went in the opposite direction toward the road in front of the cabin, wishing it were day. Though the snow had stopped last night, the sky was overcast. The snowmobile's headlight was all the illumination they had to see by.

As they rounded the cabin, Nash tried not to dwell on the occupants: one dead or near dead, the other injured and locked in the pantry.

Bitter cold penetrated his clothing and stung the portion of his face not covered by the scarf and cap. Wind brought tears to his eyes. He blinked them away and kept going. Kiera must also be suffering. Hopefully, Heather was warm enough, buried between him and Kiera.

He drove down the long driveway, the snowmobile skis gliding over the top of the loosely packed snow. White powder shot out from beneath them. It coated their shoes and the lower half of their pants.

As they descended the driveway, Nash let up on the accelerator in an attempt to slow their speed. At the bottom of the driveway, he braked before turning right. The main road lay a quarter mile ahead. From there, they'd drive to Henry Joe's garage. Ten minutes at most. And then this nightmare would finally be over.

"What's that behind us?" Kiera shouted in his ear.

Nash craned his head around to look, and the sight greeting him sent a fist of fear slamming into his gut. Three headlights came straight at them in a single file line.

Snowmobiles! Their tight formation reminded Nash of a pack of wolves on the hunt. His impression was further enhanced by the black goggles worn by the drivers, caps pulled down low over their foreheads, and clothed in thick hooded parkas. The lead snowmobile carried a passenger behind the driver.

He didn't stop to inquire if they were recreationists out for a jaunt and assumed the 7-Crowns reinforcements had arrived. He hit the gas harder.

"They're armed!" Kiera screamed.

A hasty backward glance confirmed the passenger on the lead snowmobile had leveled a rifle at them. Nash's heart bucked like a wild mustang.

"Stay down," he hollered.

They zoomed past the homes and cabins, swerving slightly on slippery patches. If they were fired at, Kiera would likely be the first one hit. And, possibly, Heather. He couldn't let that happen.

A bullet whizzed past them, much too close for comfort. Then a second one. Nash swore it grazed his cheek.

Kiera screamed again. He executed another series of zigzags but couldn't keep up the maneuvers forever. Eventually, one of those bullets would find its mark.

Dread wound through him. He fought its numbing powers. *Please*, he prayed, *don't let them encounter any innocent bystanders*. Nash couldn't bear being responsible for the loss of an innocent life.

Take the shortcut.

The voice came from both inside him and above. Divine guidance, he chose to believe. Nash hadn't used the shortcut since he and his sister were youngsters and gone on family walks. He searched for the shortcut opening, not sure he'd recognize it after all these years and in the dark.

There.

He spotted the opening between a cluster of oak trees. On the eastern horizon, a thin patch of purple revealed the first hints of a brand-new day.

The shortcut, no more than a path, was used mostly by deer and the property owners. A stream ran across the property's south border and would be frozen solid in the wake of the blizzard. On the other side of the stream, Nash could hopefully lose their pursuers in the thick woods on their race down the mountain to the main road.

If they reached the main road in one piece.

He waited until the last second before turning into the opening, wanting to give the least amount of warning. It worked. Another glance over his shoulder confirmed the lead snowmobile, the one carrying the shooter, skidded erratically while trying to make the sharp turn. The driver momentarily lost control and shot past the opening before executing a hasty U-turn. The other two vehicles slowed, and then all three continued together in rapid pursuit.

The few seconds of time Nash and Kiera gained

wasn't much. But it could make all the difference. Nash knew the terrain. They didn't.

More shots flew by them, missing by inches. God was truly watching out for Nash and Kiera and Heather. Nash increased their speed.

Watch out!

He listened to the voice and veered to the right, narrowly missing a tree stump buried beneath the snow. He'd forgotten about the stump until right then.

A few seconds later, the first snowmobile carrying the shooter hit the tree stump with a deafening crunch and enough force to launch the vehicle four feet into the air. Nash spared their pursuers a brief look and saw the shooter fly off the snowmobile right before it tipped over, landing on the driver.

Unable to stop in time, the second snowmobile collided with the first one. The driver immediately attempted to reverse, but his engine must have sustained damage, for it was sluggish and slow to respond.

Nash laid on the gas. He and Kiera weren't out of danger. The third snowmobile, several feet behind the other, was able to circumvent the mess and surged ahead.

At the property border, Nash crossed the frozen stream and entered the woods. He and Kiera still had to reach the main road, and the way there was fraught with obstacles.

The lone wolf was on their tail again and quickly gaining on them. The guy may have left his buddies behind, but he wasn't giving up. And with two people and a baby on board, Nash and Kiera were moving slower than him.

Nash pushed the snowmobile for all it had. He felt Kiera's leg muscles tense with each sharp twist and turn. She held on with that amazing determination of hers. Good thing because the going was about to get even tougher.

"Hang tight," he shouted.

Suddenly, they were flying down the mountain at a ninety-degree angle. Thick clusters of trees rushed past them on both sides. The skis on the snowmobile jumped and hitched as they skimmed over rocks and brush and whatever else lay beneath the deep snow. The absence of gunfire didn't guarantee their pursuer was unarmed.

A hundred yards. That was the remaining distance to the main road. And what then? On the smoother and flat surface of the road, their pursuer would surely overtake them before they reached Henry Joe's.

They had to leave the trail. Nash doubted he'd lose the guy, but anything was possible. Or he could hit an obstacle and end up like his friends.

"Are you okay?" Nash yelled to Kiera.

"Hurry. He's getting closer."

Her answer was good enough for him and all the motivation he needed.

They narrowly missed a towering pine tree as he veered to the right. Wind slammed into them, making steering difficult. The handlebars vibrated beneath his palms. Nash kept going, certain their pursuer was gaining on them.

Kiera's arms squeezed his waist. If they got out of this alive, he vowed to keep those arms around him always for the rest of their lives. He didn't care about witness protection. Having found her, he refused to let her go.

The ground ahead of them rose. Beyond that, it would dip drastically, and the main road would be visible. They'd made it!

As they crested the rise, the snowmobile came off the ground several inches. It sank upon landing before finding traction. Both Nash and Kiera were nearly unseated. Nash didn't wait for them to regain their balance before pressing on.

Their skis momentarily lost traction upon hitting the road. But then, with no obstacles beneath them, they soared ahead of their pursuer. Not for long. He reached the road and chased after them like a heat-seeking missile.

Nash leaned forward over the snowmobile's handlebars, willing the machine for more speed. The next second, a bullet sailed past them. Nash risked a backward glance. The guy steered his snowmobile one-handed, pointing a gun at them with the other.

"Don't let go," Nash yelled to Kiera.

He leaned into the curve and prayed their pursuer would need both hands to manage the challenging terrain and not shoot at them. With God on their side, they'd make it to Henry Joe's garage ahead of their pursuer.

They came out of the curve at full speed. Everything around them blurred. The landscape became a swirling collage of gray colors and shapes in the emerging light of dawn. He almost didn't notice the vehicles at first and, when he did, he couldn't believe his eyes.

There, parked on the road near the marshal's disabled car, sat a county vehicle with a large snowplow attached to the front. Behind that sat a sheriff's SUV. Two men stood near the marshal's car. Nash recognized the county worker, a regular in Wild Wind Hills. The one in deputy's uniform held the scarf Nash had tied to the fender. Both men looked up, visibly startled, as Nash and Kiera roared toward them.

An overwhelming sensation of relief swept through him as he slowed. Behind him, he felt Kiera shift in the seat.

"He's leaving," she shouted, exuberance in her voice instead of fear.

Nash couldn't resist and looked, too. Indeed, their pursuer was hightailing it away from them. Nash doubted he'd be found, but that didn't matter to him. He, Kiera, and Heather had reached safety. A lump of gratitude formed in his throat. He swallowed it down as he braked to a stop near the county snowplow and cut the engine.

"Nash, is that you?" Randy, the county worker, hurried toward them. "We found your mom's scarf and were wondering what happened."

The deputy, a middle-aged man with an air of experience, asked, "Are you all right? What's going on?"

"We've had some trouble." Nash turned and helped Kiera and Heather off the snowmobile. "That guy chasing us has a gun and tried to kill us. There are three more a half mile back in the woods. One has a rifle. They won't stick around for long."

Instantly, the deputy pressed the radio transmitter attached to his shoulder and put in a call, alerting the dispatcher as to the situation and requesting assistance.

"We need an ambulance, too." Nash said, holding onto Kiera's arm. Her legs wobbled unsteadily. "There's a US marshal in my cabin on the kitchen floor. She's injured. Badly. The man who shot her is an operative for the 7-Crowns Syndicate and also injured. He's bound and locked in the pantry. Assuming he's still there and didn't escape. The four chasing us probably also work for the 7-Crowns."

"What the—" The deputy sent Nash a look before relaying the information to the dispatcher. He'd have questions for Nash when he finished. Plenty of them. Nash thanked God he and Kiera were alive and able to answer them.

His limbs stiff, he lifted his good leg and climbed off the snowmobile. Pain exploded in his injured leg. He'd forgotten all about his wound during the chase.

"Good grief, Nash." Randy moved closer. "Are you okay, pal? That's a lot of blood."

Nash glanced down at his pants. As he did, his head swam and the pain intensified. "Kiera…" Unable to stand, he collapsed to the ground, the adrenaline that had kept him going fading.

"Nash!"

Kiera's face materialized through the haze surrounding him. He vaguely heard the deputy tell the dispatcher, "We need another ambulance ASAP. I have a shooting victim."

Chapter Thirteen

"What's taking so long?" Kiera asked for the third time.

She sat in the back seat of Randy's truck, bouncing a crying Heather on her lap. Beside her, Nash stretched out as much as possible in the cramped space, his injured leg elevated and propped on the front seat. The blasting heater warmed the vehicle's interior. It did nothing to relieve Kiera's anxiety.

"They'll be along soon as they can, ma'am," Randy said from the front seat.

A jovial fellow with a cherub face and ready smile, she'd liked him immediately. She liked him even more when he offered his phone to Nash so he could call his parents. Nash told them very little, refusing to worry them. He said he'd been hurt, would be fine, that he loved them and to meet him at the hospital.

Even though the blizzard had abated late yesterday, weather conditions continued to be problematic. Response times were taking much longer than usual. Two ambulances had been sent ahead to the cabin, one for the marshal and the other for the operative. They were only capable of transporting one patient at a time. A third ambulance was en route for Nash.

He'd insisted he could wait. Kiera hadn't been able to convince him otherwise and that he should go ahead of the operative. Her guess was he wanted the operative in custody as soon as possible.

"How's the bleeding?" he asked.

She lifted the cloth covering his wound. "The same."

"Not bad, then."

"Be serious."

He grinned at her.

Randy had produced an impressively stocked first-aid kit. Between him and Kiera, they'd wrestled an unsteady Nash into the back seat of Randy's vehicle while the deputy took off on Nash's snowmobile to the cabin. Once Nash was settled, Kiera had applied a thick pad of gauze from the first-aid kit to his thigh, taped it as best she could and then used a clean disposable windshield wipe from Randy's store of emergency supplies to apply pressure.

Her concern for infection was alleviated by the knowledge he'd soon be receiving antibiotics at the hospital.

"You could bleed out before help gets here," she said.

"I'm not going to bleed out, Kiera." He squeezed her hand. "It's a flesh wound."

"It's a bullet wound."

"And nowhere near a vital organ or a vein."

"You're no doctor." She made a face but squeezed his fingers in return, thankful they were all alive and safe.

Dearest Lord. Once again, You have led me through

the valley of the shadow of death to the other side. I am eternally grateful.

"More coffee, Nash?" Randy asked. He'd offered them both a cup from his thermos. Only Nash had accepted.

"Thanks."

Randy refilled the paper cup. Seemed he was quite accustomed to helping out stranded people and came prepared. No sooner had they gotten Nash into the vehicle, than he'd radioed Henry Joe, who'd arrived in a jiffy with his personal snowplow to clear the road in order that the ambulances and backup deputy sheriffs could reach the cabin.

Of the three deputies who responded, one had stayed behind to question Nash and Kiera and await the third ambulance. Also to meet the US Marshals on their way from Flagstaff. As of right now, neither Kiera nor Nash had any idea what the deputies had encountered in the cabin.

"Would your little one like a snack?" Randy asked Kiera and offered an open sleeve of crackers from where he sat in the driver's seat.

"Thank you." Kiera removed four crackers and gave Heather two, one for each chubby fist. She immediately stuffed them into her mouth.

The deputy waiting behind with them appeared at the rear passenger window and motioned for Kiera to lower it, which she did.

"How much longer until the ambulance arrives?" Kiera asked. "He really needs medical attention."

"They're doing their best," the young woman deputy said. "The ambulance is coming from Flagstaff."

"There aren't any available in Camp Verde?"

"All of them are on calls. Been a crazy morning. Four-car traffic accident. Heart attack victim. A floor heater malfunctioned and caught a trailer on fire."

Kiera tried not to let her frustrations get the best of her. These people were in desperate need, too. But what if Nash suffered permanent damage to his leg? Or, she couldn't bear the thought, died from his injury?

"It's going to be all right, hon," he said softly.

Softly or weakly? There was a difference.

Suddenly, the deputy straightened. "Here they come."

Kiera strained to see. Nash tried to sit up.

"Don't hurt yourself," she warned, well aware he wouldn't listen to her.

The first ambulance came toward them down the freshly plowed road. It was followed by a deputy sheriff SUV and the second ambulance. Another deputy sheriff SUV brought up the rear. Kiera assumed at least one deputy had remained at the cabin, securing it for the crime scene investigators.

"Do you think she's still alive?" Kiera asked in a hushed voice. She imagined the marshal was in the first ambulance for no reason other than it made sense given the lineup of vehicles.

The deputy said nothing.

"They have the sirens on," Randy commented.

She understood his meaning. If the marshal weren't alive, there'd be no reason to rush. "That's good."

Despite the marshal's betrayal, Kiera wanted her to live. Nash was right; the marshal had been put in an impossible situation. She deserved some sympathy.

As the first ambulance drove past them, Kiera tried

to read the expression on the driver's face—to no avail. He sat alone in the front, concentrating on the road ahead while simultaneously talking on his radio. His partner must be in the back with the patient.

After them came the first deputy sheriff SUV.

"Is that him?" Kiera asked when the second ambulance approached and, again, got no answer.

She pictured the operative handcuffed to the gurney and shouting angrily at the EMT attending him. Maybe one of the deputies was in the ambulance with him. She had no clue how any of that worked.

When the last SUV had passed, their deputy stepped aside to talk on her radio. She returned a short time later.

"The ambulance will be here in about fifteen minutes."

Fifteen minutes. As much as Kiera wanted Nash to get to a hospital, she hated the thought of being parted from him.

"How are you doing?" the deputy asked Nash.

"All right. I've been hurt worse tripping in a gopher hole."

What was with all the He-Man stuff? A gunshot wound was nothing like tripping in a gopher hole.

"Can you tell us anything?" Nash used his elbow to prop himself up to a half-sitting position.

The deputy considered a moment, then said, "The perp was located in the pantry. He sustained several injuries, a possible punctured lung and likely concussion, but is expected to recover and face charges."

"Is he talking?"

She shook her head. "No, and he won't. He's already lawyered up."

"What about the marshal?" Kiera asked. "Did she survive?"

"I'm told she's in and out of consciousness. That's all I know."

Kiera nodded. Maybe when her escort from the US Marshals' office arrived, they'd tell her more.

"I have to say—" the deputy gave Kiera and Nash an admiring once-over "—I'm pretty impressed with you two. That was quite a feat you pulled off. Crawling through the tunnel, laying false tracks, climbing the porch roof and hiding in the cubby. Overpowering the perp and escaping on a snowmobile with a baby in tow. And with you injured." She indicated Nash's leg. "A great story to tell your grandkids."

Their grandkids. Except Kiera would be heading to Dallas very soon and never see Nash again. He must have read her thoughts, as he reached for her hand again.

"Nash is the one who saved us," she said, her voice cracking. "He was amazing."

His tender smile sent her heart soaring and broke it in half at the same time. She couldn't ask him to give up everything and everyone he loved and go into witness protection with her. But how could she part from him?

"You ever consider going into law enforcement?" Randy asked Nash with a broad grin. "You're a natural."

"I'm happy working for the Department of Agriculture. And I'm not sure my blood pressure could take it."

In the distance, a siren whined.

"Sounds like your ride is here," the deputy said and stepped away.

The moment Kiera dreaded had arrived. Yes, Nash had said he wanted to see her when everything was over and assured her they'd find a way to be together. But that had been wishful thinking. Their emotions talking rather than their heads.

Heather started to cry. Kiera gave her another cracker, but she tossed it on the floor. Kiera bent and retrieved the cracker, stuffing it in her pocket for lack of a better place.

Randy opened the front door. "I need to…talk to the deputy or whatever."

He was granting them some privacy. Kiera could have hugged him if she weren't on the verge of tears.

Nash lowered his elevated leg and struggled to a sitting position.

"What are you doing?"

"I hate the thought of leaving you."

"I hate it, too."

He attempted to scoot closer to her. Kiera put a hand on his knee to stop him and did the scooting instead, closing the distance between them until they were side by side.

He placed an arm around her shoulders. "When will I see you again?"

"Nash. I told you. I have to testify. After that, I have no idea what will happen. If the 7-Crowns is still targeting me, which is likely, I'll have to relocate. I may stay in Dallas under the US Marshals' protection."

"Do you still have my number?"

She patted the front of her coat. The slip of paper he'd given her earlier was in her shirt pocket. "Yes."

"Call me. First chance you get."

The sound of the siren grew louder.

"I will."

"I'm serious, hon."

"I'll call." But that was all she could promise, and he knew it. She could tell from the sorrow in his eyes.

"I'll wait for you," he said. "No matter how long."

"I can't ask that of you."

"You're not asking."

He pressed his forehead to hers, and she felt his sadness flow into her and mingle with her own.

"I've never met anyone like you," she said when they pulled apart.

"Don't quit on us. God has a plan. Have faith."

She believed God had a plan for her and Nash both. She just wasn't sure that plan involved the two of them spending the rest of their lives together. Not when it would put all of them in danger, along with Nash's family. That was a risk Kiera wasn't ready to take. She had enough trouble keeping herself and Heather safe.

To her surprise, Nash leaned forward and kissed the top of Heather's head. "Take care of your mom for me, squirt. See you soon."

Kiera was going to miss his easy and natural way with her daughter. She was going to miss so many things about him.

The ambulance arrived and parked behind Randy's snowplow. Kiera and Nash had less than a minute left.

"Remember me," she whispered to Nash and held him close. If it were possible to make time stand still, she would. Only she couldn't, and a moment later, the EMTs appeared at the window.

"What's going on?" the older, stouter one asked with

exaggerated cheer. "Heard you got yourself in a little jam."

Unable to help herself, Kiera began to cry softly.

"Shh. Don't." Nash brought her hand to his lips like he had in the cubby.

Randy opened the rear passenger door on Nash's side. The EMTs brought the gurney to the door.

"Give me a second." Nash reached under his coat into his jeans pocket. He withdrew the gold cross he'd taken from a drawer in the bedroom yesterday and pressed it into Kiera's hand. "This was my mom's. She gave it to my dad when he enlisted in the army. Told him it would keep him safe and to bring it home to her."

"Oh, Nash. I can't take this."

"Come home to me, Kiera. Bring the cross."

Tears filled her eyes.

"We've got to go," the stouter EMT said.

Nash nodded at Kiera and then swung his legs out and onto the running board.

"Easy now," the younger EMT said. "Let us do the work."

"I can walk," Nash insisted and did a poor job of hiding his pain.

"Company policy," the EMT joked.

Kiera put the cross in her pocket. Later, she'd fasten it around her neck.

Once the EMTs had Nash on the gurney, things happened fast. Too fast. Kiera had trouble keeping up. One EMT took Nash's vitals while the other one cut away his jeans to expose the bullet wound, which they then treated. An IV was started at some point, and they attached a monitor that beeped and buzzed. They asked lots of questions.

Next thing Kiera knew, he was lifted onto the gurney. Randy came over to say goodbye, shake Nash's hand and wish him well.

"I'll be in touch," Nash told him.

"Counting on it."

The EMTs started pushing the gurney.

He's leaving!

The words were like a shout inside Kiera's head. Without thinking, she scrambled out of the vehicle and trotted to catch up with them. Heather objected to the bumpy ride.

"Hold on. I need to talk to him."

The EMTs stopped. "Make it fast," the stouter one said.

She rushed to Nash's side and buried her face in his neck. "Stay safe."

"I wish you could come with me. Nothing I'd like better than to see you first thing when I come out of surgery."

"Nothing I'd like better than to be there."

"Soon, Kiera."

"Soon." Not a lie. A fervent hope.

She walked alongside Nash to the ambulance, clutching his hand. There was so much she wanted to say and no time to say it. His touch conveyed that he felt the same.

The deputy appeared at her side. "Ma'am, the marshals are here."

Kiera looked up to see an unmarked sedan rolling toward them. Nash's hand abruptly slipped from hers.

She spun just as the EMTs were lifting him into the ambulance.

"Goodbye," she called.

If he answered her, the sound of the EMT closing the doors drowned it out.

This was not how Nash had intended to spend Christmas day. The big breakfast with his parents followed by opening gifts, yes. Delivering holiday care packages to Wild Wind Hills residents in need like Mrs. Smithson, sure. And their traditional turkey dinner had been served at one o'clock sharp like always.

But Nash had hoped to hear from Kiera by now. He'd held on to the hope she and Heather would be part of the Myers' holiday celebration right up until dinnertime. Now, he stood on his crutches at the living room window, scrolling through his phone's call log and scanning news sites. Unlike during the blizzard, he had excellent service.

If only she'd call.

From his hospital bed, he'd insisted his parents search the cabin for his and Kiera's phones. They'd found the phones, but the SIM cards had been removed. On the day of his release, he'd refused to return to the cabin until his parents drove him to the nearest phone store. The clerk was able to restore Nash's phone. There was no voice mail from Kiera.

Why hadn't he thought to give her his mom and dad's phone numbers, too?

During his three-day hospital stay, he'd been interviewed by the US Marshals' office, the FBI and the Sheriff's Department. None of the agencies had given him information regarding Kiera and no amount of pleading on his part had made any difference. They didn't care that Nash had nearly died at the hands of a 7-Crowns operative or played a significant role in capturing their operative and keeping their star witness alive. He'd also tried the Flagstaff police with the same frustrating results.

"Sorry, Mr. Myers. We're not allowed to discuss the details of an ongoing investigation."

"The agent or deputy or officer, take your pick, will be in touch."

And his least favorite, "Give me your name and number, and someone will get back to you."

Only no one ever called him. And if he heard one more cool, clipped, impersonal, unhelpful voice, he'd toss his phone against the nearest wall. But then what if Kiera tried to call him? He prayed she and Heather were all right and wondered if Kiera had testified against The Chairman yet. Did she think about him as much as he was thinking about her?

With the cabin's satellite dish repaired, Nash had conducted endless searches on his parents' laptop, seeking information related to the trial in Dallas and the 7-Crowns Syndicate. There wasn't much to be found, perhaps because of the holidays. A news article he'd located two days ago mentioned the court taking a break and resuming after the first of the year. He took that as an indication Kiera had testified. So, where were she and Heather, and what were they doing? Not knowing was making him restless.

"Sweetheart, come sit down," his mom said and patted the couch cushion next to her. "You must be tired."

"I will. In a minute."

"All that standing isn't good for your leg."

"I'm fine, Mom."

"Are you?" She gazed across the room at him with a worried expression that reminded Nash of the one he'd seen staring back at him from the mirror for the last six days. "The doctor said you need to rest."

He was supposed to, if not rest, at least be taking it easy. Not standing by the window for hours on the slim chance Kiera appeared in the driveway.

Giving up, he hobbled over to the couch, leaned his crutches against the side table and sat down next to his mom. "You're the one who should be resting," he said, setting his phone within easy reach. "You've been working hard all week. Today, especially. The dinner you and dad made was incredible."

"I'm fine, son," she echoed his previous response to her with a smile.

They really were a lot alike.

His dad entered and went to the fireplace where he added a fresh log from the holder. Finishing, he stood and stretched. "Is it four already? Anyone in the mood for hot chocolate?"

Hot chocolate reminded Nash of that first night with Kiera when the two of them had chatted right here in this room. The fire poker reminded him of when she'd wielded it like a fierce warrior in defense of her young child.

It would be like this always, he supposed. Memories were everywhere, waiting to be stirred.

"We'd love some hot chocolate," his mom said, answering for herself and Nash. "The perfect remedy for a chilly afternoon."

Nash's dad returned to the kitchen. He and Nash's mom wore matching holiday sweaters, as they frequently did. The ones today featured Christmas tree lights.

He'd always considered it kind of corny. Now, he thought about growing older with Kiera and the two of them wearing matching holiday sweaters. It was a nice way of proclaiming to the world, "We're together." He could think of worse things.

"You'll hear from her soon." His mom reached up and brushed the hair from his face as if he were a small boy. "I have faith."

He nodded, afraid to speak lest his emotions betray him. What if, when Kiera did finally contact him, it was to say a final goodbye?

"The two of you went through a lot together. That creates a bond not easily broken."

She wasn't kidding.

"You'll find each other again. I'm sure of it. God didn't bring you together simply to separate you so soon. He has a plan."

"That's pretty much what I told Kiera."

"She'll come back to you, son. You just need to be patient."

He thought of the cross he'd given her. Kiera hadn't sounded like she was coming back to him when they'd parted at the ambulance.

"I hope so," he said.

"I *know* so."

His mom had been intensely optimistic since learning about Kiera. She wanted her son to be reunited with the woman who, in the span of a few days, had so completely won his affections, convinced Kiera must be *the one*. And she was right. Nash had met his soul mate the day he rescued Kiera from the blizzard.

When he'd told his parents the story of those days with Kiera and their ordeal, he'd left out his initial attraction and then growing feelings for her. But his mother, with her keen perception, had immediately insisted on learning more about this woman he'd escaped certain death with, cumulating with a hair-raising snowmobile chase.

"We've been through this," he said. "She doesn't want me to give up my life in order follow her into witness protection." He resisted picking up his phone. There'd be no new text message or missed-call notification. "Whether or not I'm willing isn't the issue. She has to agree and let me follow her into the program."

His mom sighed. "I'd never stop you from being with someone you loved. But I'd hate never seeing you again and miss you terribly. I'd also be glad you found your someone special."

Nash's dad returned, carrying three mugs of hot chocolate, which he passed around before sitting in the rocker. The rocker Kiera had frequently occupied with Heather. Another memory surfaced in Nash's mind and lingered.

He must have heard part of Nash's conversation with his mom for he asked, "Is it possible Kiera could move someplace closer to us than Fresno? That way, you could arrange to meet. On the lowdown, naturally."

What kind of relationship would that be? A stolen

few hours here and there. Asking Kiera to accept those restrictions seemed unfair.

"She's worried the 7-Crowns Syndicate will come after me and our family and kill us as a way to get revenge on her."

His dad sipped his hot chocolate and considered. "Does the 7-Crowns care about what you did to their operative?"

Nash shook his head. "He's basically a hired gun. Not a leader of the organization like the man she's testifying against."

"What if Mom and I moved nearer your sister? She wants to spend more time with the new grandbaby."

"That wouldn't stop the 7-Crowns from finding you. They have long arms and a lot of dangerous people working for them. They don't believe in letting bygones be bygones. More like an eye for an eye."

His mom shuddered. "I can't believe what they did to Kiera's husband. I don't care if he was stealing. He didn't deserve to die. And that poor woman, having to witness it."

"She's strong," his dad said. "I wouldn't have the courage to testify against the 7-Crowns. Especially if I had a youngster. Takes a special person with a lot of conviction."

"She may not have testified yet." Nash set aside his half-finished hot chocolate, a dull ache in his chest. All this talking, all the memories, all the reminders of why he and Kiera couldn't be together had drained him. "None of the news articles mention her specifically."

"The prosecution could be protecting her identity," his mom offered.

"As they should," his dad agreed.

A silence fell over them, which lasted several moments. Nash's mom broke it with a suggestion.

"I don't think it would hurt to say a prayer." She took hold of Nash's hand. "What do you think?"

"Certainly can't hurt," his dad said and bowed his head over his clasped hands.

"Dearest Lord," Nash's mom began. "We ask you to watch over Kiera and sweet little Heather. Give Kiera the strength she needs for the difficult journey she's on and the days ahead. Protect her and Heather from danger, as you did before when the 7-Crowns operatives were after them and Nash. And should you see fit, please reunite Kiera and Nash. We know we're asking a lot of you. But these two people, your most devoted servants, truly care for each other. If they're not meant to be together, we'll do our best to understand and accept Your will. Whatever's to be, please give Kiera and Heather a life of peace and comfort. Amen."

"Amen," Nash's dad said.

Nash added a few silent words of his own before murmuring, "Amen."

His mom sniffed and pulled a tissue from inside the sleeve of her sweater. Dabbing her nose, she changed the subject, saying, "I was thinking of knitting a blanket for Victoria's baby. My hands have been good lately. The new meds are helping. Maybe in maroon and gold, Arizona State University colors. Do you think she and Ben would like that? That's where they met."

"They'll love it." Nash's dad stood. As he did, they heard the sound of an approaching vehicle. He peered out the window. "Huh. Looks like we have a visitor."

Nash's pulse kicked into high gear. He cautioned himself to remain calm. Visitors to the cabin were common, especially on a holiday.

"Must be the Conroys." Nash's mom braced a hand on the couch arm and rose with visible stiffness. "They weren't home when we stopped by earlier."

Nash stood with equal stiffness and reached for his crutches.

"Odd," his dad mused. "It's a gray sedan. The Conroys drive a minivan."

Nash hobbled to the window. What were the chances? None, he told himself as he tried to discern the occupants. Other people besides US marshals drove gray sedans.

It came to a stop in front of the carport. Late afternoon sunlight glinted off the tinted windows. Gaging by the movements inside, there were two occupants. In the front, anyway. Nash had no view of the back seat.

In the yard, pine trees stood like majestic giants, their tops and boughs covered with snow. Sun glinted off the white landscape, turning it a vivid gold.

The setting couldn't have been more perfect for what he saw next. Both front doors opened and a pair of men emerged, their authoritative demeanor and navy coats instantly identifying them as law enforcement. The one on the left opened the rear passenger side door and out stepped a much smaller figure, clearly female, bundled from head to toe.

Nash didn't need to see her face. His heart instantly recognized her and shouted with joy.

"Who is it?" his mom inquired, coming up behind him.

Nash didn't answer. He leaned down, kissed her

cheek and hurried as fast as he could on crutches to the front door. Flinging it open, he went outside. By then, the woman's upper half had disappeared back inside the vehicle.

The two men gave Nash a steely once-over as he approached—one nodded curtly, the other pleasantly.

"Mr. Myers, I presume?" the curt one said.

Nash didn't answer him, either. He made straight for the car, mindless of the frigid cold and his lack of a coat. When Kiera withdrew and straightened, she held a pink-faced Heather in her arms.

Seeing him, she broke into a smile of profound happiness. "Nash. You're here."

He dropped one crutch and reached out an arm for her and Heather. She went to him, and he enveloped the two of them in a fierce embrace. Now that he had them, he wasn't letting go. Ever.

Chapter Fourteen

"Come in, come in." Nash's mom, the woman could be none other given her resemblance to Nash, called to Kiera and the US marshals from the front porch. Standing beside her, and wearing a matching sweater, stood a man that must be Nash's dad.

"Welcome," he bellowed. "And Merry Christmas."

Kiera swallowed the lump in her throat. Not making a complete fool of herself by bursting into tears was difficult. For the past six days, whenever the trial hadn't consumed her every thought, she'd pictured herself seeing Nash again and being comforted in his arms. Only yesterday had she learned her ardent wish would become a reality. And now, she was here.

Thank you, Lord, for this day.

"My folks would love to meet you and Heather," Nash said.

He'd yet to let go of her. The weight of his arm around her felt wonderful—secure without being possessive. She almost didn't want to move. But meeting his parents was an unexpected pleasure she couldn't pass up.

"Of course," she said and grabbed the diaper bag. "I'd love nothing better."

"You shouldn't stand outside, ma'am," Marshal Kline said. "Just in case." He tended to be a stickler.

Marshal Redding, not so much. "Give them a minute. They missed each other."

Kiera and Nash exchanged amused glances at that.

Both marshals had introduced themselves and shown Nash their identification. They hadn't asked Nash to identify himself. She supposed their fierce embrace had been enough to satisfy them.

Using one crutch, he led the way into the house. Kiera supported his other side. She wasn't ready to let go of him. Marshal Redding brought the crutch Nash had dropped.

"It's so nice to finally meet you," Kiera said to Nash's parents as she and the marshals handed over their coats. "Nash has told me so many nice things about you."

"He told me nice things about you, too." The other woman beamed, her attention focused on the baby. "Is this Heather? She's adorable."

Kiera spoke in a high-pitched baby voice as she turned Heather toward Nash's mom. "Say hello to Mrs. Myers."

"Oh, please. Call me Ginny."

"And I'm Ben," Nash's dad added. He, too, appeared smitten with Heather.

"Can I hold her?" Ginny asked tentatively. "I love babies, and Nash's sister is expecting."

"I heard." Kiera sent Nash a look, remembering their

conversation. "And yes, you can hold her. Though she can be a little standoffish with strangers. Don't take it personally."

"Let me sit down first." Ginny started toward the living room. "I'm not always steady on my feet."

Nash remained close to Kiera as they followed his mom. Once she was seated in the rocking chair, Kiera handed over Heather. Rather than cry or stiffen, she stared curiously up at this new person and promptly reached up to grab her glasses.

"I'm sorry." Kiera started forward. "She's really curious."

Ginny waved her away. "It's no problem." Displaying the ease of someone experienced with babies, she removed her glasses and set them aside. She then amused Heather with a plastic reindeer sitting nearby. Heather was entranced. They both were. Ginny, Kiera decided, was a natural grandmother.

She turned to Nash. "I think your mom has a new friend."

"She loves babies." The gratitude shining in his eyes tugged at her heartstrings.

Kiera touched his arm, wanting, needing to be alone with him. "Is there somewhere we can talk in private? The marshals really are on a schedule."

Ben must have heard them, or picked up the gist of their subdued conversation, for he suddenly announced, "Gentlemen, may I offer you some pie and coffee? Homemade cherry or pumpkin. Your choice, and the coffee's fresh."

"Why not?" Marshal Redding shrugged at his partner.

"I'll come, too," Ginny blurted. "I could use a pick-me-up."

Kiera saw right through Ginny's excuse—through all the excuses—and nodded her appreciation.

"Maybe I can take this little rascal for you." Ben lifted Heather who, after a quick squeak of surprise, was completely enthralled by his beard. "Hey, you, that hurts," he complained humorously and then helped Nash's mom out of the rocking chair, which Kiera thought was sweet.

She walked to the kitchen on her own but with a noticeable awkwardness to her gait. The marshals went along, debating whipped cream versus ice cream.

When Kiera and Nash were alone, he gestured to the couch. "Let's sit."

Confident her baby was in good hands, Kiera did, thrilled when he leaned his crutches against the coffee table and settled right next to her. Not two cushions away.

Folding her hand inside his, he asked, "How was the trial?"

"Hard." She drew in a breath. "Terrifying. Intimidating. Nerve-racking."

"Is it over?"

"Yes, I'm happy to say."

"Was The Chairman found guilty?"

"It didn't get that far. He accepted a plea agreement right before closing arguments."

"Really?"

She scrunched her mouth to the side. "How did the prosecution put it? There was a preponderance of evidence. Mine wasn't the only eyewitness testimony, though I didn't know that until I arrived in Dallas. Footage surfaced from one of those doorbell cameras on the house across the street. Images of three men entering our side yard. Though not a positive ID, the general height and body shape matched The Chairman's. The time stamp on the video also coincided with my call to 9-1-1. A woman two houses away heard the gunshot and posted it on one of those neighborhood apps. A security camera in a parking lot less than five miles from our house recorded The Chairman and two men getting into a vehicle twenty minutes before the murder."

"Lots of little things, but I guess they all add up to prove your accounting."

"Not prove. More like support. DNA and ballistic evidence would have been better. But now it's not needed."

"What changed The Chairman's mind?"

"Something new came to light while the marshal and I were stranded here at the cabin. It goes to motive. I was in shock when the Marshals' office told me."

"Told you what?"

Kiera couldn't suppress the rise of emotions in her. "Nash." She squeezed his hands. "I can leave witness protection if I want. I'll have to continue maintaining a low profile. No running for public office or writing a tell-all book. But I won't be a prisoner in my own house, scared to even go to the grocery store."

"I don't understand. Isn't the 7-Crowns after you?"

"Not anymore. According to the FBI, The Chairman was actually the one embezzling from the syndicate. He brought in Joshua as his partner."

"Partner?"

"He might have forced Joshua into it to cover his

tracks. We'll probably never know for sure. Apparently, someone in the 7-Crowns figured out funds had gone missing and reported it to the head of the organization. Rather than risk being discovered and executed as a traitor, The Chairman killed Joshua before he could talk and laid the blame on him. The head of the 7-Crowns bought The Chairman's story and protected him until recently when one of his men turned against him."

"No honor among thieves."

"I guess not." Kiera inched closer to Nash. "The thing is the 7-Crowns is now targeting The Chairman. Not me. The FBI is concerned the 7-Crowns will make a move against him while he's in jail, awaiting the end of the trial. Which is why he took the plea agreement. That way, he can be moved to a maximum-security prison and placed under twenty-four-hour surveillance. Even then, his life will be in danger. The 7-Crowns can get to him in prison."

Nash's brows knit together. "I want justice to prevail and The Chairman to pay for what he did. I don't like the idea of the 7-Crowns taking revenge on him."

"No," Kiera agreed.

"He certainly knew what would happen to him if the 7-Crowns discovered him embezzling."

"He must have believed he could get away with it. And he did until he was betrayed by one of his henchmen."

"Wow." Nash shook his head. "That's a lot to take in all at once."

She nodded. "I'm still grappling with it."

"Have you heard anything about Marshal Gifford? I was told she survived. Nothing more."

"Her children are fine. They're safe with their father. She's no longer a marshal."

"Are they going to charge her?"

"I'm not sure. I do know she's cooperating with both the FBI and the US Marshals' office."

"Let's hope they cut her some slack," Nash said. "She did try to defend us in the end. She couldn't help that she hit me instead of the operative."

"I'm glad you're all right. Very glad."

Kiera leaned in, and Nash wrapped his arms around her.

"Me, too. If only for this."

"I've missed you," she whispered.

"I was hoping you'd call." He nuzzled her cheek with his. "This is much better."

Kiera wasn't sure what lay in store for them. Nash had talked about wanting to see her again, but that was during their ordeal when their emotions were running high and they were scared for their lives. He could feel differently now. But considering the way he held her, she doubted it. She'd made up her mind before coming here today—if he was willing to give them a try, then so was she.

"I don't have to stay in Fresno," she ventured.

"Dad was just talking about that before you got here."

"He was?"

"Yeah. He suggested you could move to Flagstaff. Or Camp Verde."

"Hmm. Camp Verde. I hadn't considered that," she teased, having considered it frequently these past few days. Small-town living appealed to her. Very much.

"I have to be honest," Nash said. "There aren't a lot of job opportunities. Unless you're willing to commute."

"That's not a problem. I work from home." An idea suddenly occurred to her. "Maybe I can find a job in my old field."

"Data architect, right?"

"You remembered."

"I can't wait to learn more about you."

"Well, my favorite food is Italian. Medical TV dramas are my guilty pleasure. I'm an only child. And I played the flute in marching band four straight years in high school."

"Can you still play?"

She grinned. "I'll save that tidbit for later."

"You can tell me over dinner. There's a great Italian restaurant in Flagstaff. And it's family friendly. We can bring Heather."

"I'm glad you mentioned her." Kiera let her gaze rove his face, searching for any sign of reluctance. "Because we're a package deal."

"I wouldn't have it any other way."

"My parents are also part of the deal."

"Do you think they'll like me?"

"They'll adore you." Like she did.

"Are they coming out for a visit?"

"Seriously? I can't keep them away. We had our first video chat yesterday."

"How'd that go?"

"Mom cried."

"Only your mom?"

"No." Kiera grinned sheepishly. "They're planning on meeting me in Flagstaff a week from tomorrow, which is the soonest they can get off work and hire a pet sitter. We'll all drive out together to Fresno and move my stuff from the condo." The only question had been move to where? Now Kiera had her answer. "That'll give me a chance to find a place in Camp Verde. What's the housing situation there?"

"As it so happens, I have a month off from work. Sick leave. I can show you around."

"I'd like that."

"Tomorrow? We can have that dinner afterward."

She laughed again, not caring that Nash was willing to move fast. "I'll rent a car and then pick you up here."

"I'll get my parents to drive me. They won't mind."

Suddenly contrite, Kiera said, "I'm sorry I didn't call before. I couldn't."

"I understand."

He probably did because Nash was like that.

"I can go with you and your family to Fresno, if you want, and help you move."

"What about your leg?"

"I'll supervise." He tugged on one of her curls. "Let you do the heavy lifting."

"I may take you up on that offer." An idea occurred to her. "Would your parents maybe like to come to Flagstaff for the day and meet my parents?"

He pulled her close for a hug. "I know they would."

She sighed with contentment. "I've been thinking a lot these last couple of days and asking God for an answer. Some kind of sign. He gave me one."

"What was it?"

"You. When you came out onto the porch, and I saw

the look on your face, I knew. I'm supposed to be with you, wherever you are."

"Good." He took her chin between his fingers and tilted her face to his. It seemed to Kiera he saw inside her to the center of her heart. "Because I'm falling in love with you. Yeah, it's soon. But I am."

She silently replayed the words she'd longed to hear over and over. "I'm glad. Because I'm falling in love with you, too. I wouldn't move and start over, again, if I wasn't convinced we're right for each other."

"That's all I need to hear."

They might have kissed, only they were interrupted by Nash's parents and the marshals returning from the kitchen. Ben carried Heather while Ginny played an I've-got-your-nose game with her.

"Apologies for the interruption," Marshal Kline, the stickler, said. "We need to leave. It's getting dark."

"Right." Kiera tried to hide her disappointment, but she was sure it showed on her face.

"Hey, I have an idea," Nash said. "Do you have to return with the marshals? Can you catch a different ride later?"

Her gaze traveled between the two men. "I... Do I?"

"You're free to stay, ma'am, if that's what you're asking."

"Well." She returned to face Nash, excitement building.

"My folks and I can drive you back to Flagstaff."

"Are you sure?"

"Yes," Ben answered for Nash and put an arm on his wife's shoulder. "That way you can stay, and we can all get to know each other better."

"If you want, we can look at places online to rent,"

Nash suggested. "Make a list for tomorrow. And maybe," he glanced at his parents, "I could get a hotel room so Kiera wouldn't have to drive back here tomorrow."

"That's fine with us," Ben answered, and Ginny nodded.

"Okay." Kiera smiled at the ease with which everything had fallen into place. "Sounds like a plan."

She walked the marshals outside and bid them goodbye on the porch. They wished her well before jogging across the yard to the car, Marshal Kline already on the phone.

When she returned to the living room, she found Nash waiting for her right where she'd left him on the couch.

"Everything okay?" he asked as she sat.

"Yes." She looked around the room. "Great."

Ginny occupied the rocking chair, Heather on her lap. Ben stood beside them, making funny faces that delighted Heather.

Kiera suffered a pang of homesickness. She wished her parents lived closer, but that wasn't possible. Not until they retired. Seeing her daughter with the Myerses, however, warmed her insides. This loving and generous couple wouldn't replace Kiera's parents. Never. But they would enrich Heather's life. A child couldn't have enough people who cared about them. People like Nash, who would be a great father figure. Maybe, one day, Heather would be his daughter for real. And have a little brother or sister.

"This has been the absolute best Christmas ever," Ginny said, her face radiant.

Ben told Kiera, "You already feel like part of the family."

Had he heard her and Nash talking or simply guessed? Anyone who looked at them could probably tell they were head over heels in love.

For the next forty-five minutes, they chatted. Kiera thoroughly enjoyed hearing the childhood stories about Nash and his sister. She told them all about growing up in Connecticut, which, in some ways, wasn't that different from Wild Wind Hills. No one mentioned the ordeal with the marshal and the operative. Kiera supposed they'd talk about it one day, but now wasn't the time.

At one point, Heather became fussy. Kiera took her from Ginny before the baby began crying in earnest and gave her a bottle from the diaper bag. When she finished, full of energy and raring to go, Kiera let her explore on the couch while the grown-ups continued their lively conversation.

"Who's hungry?" Ben eventually asked and rose from the recliner where he'd been sitting. "There's plenty of leftovers."

"We should eat before the drive," Ginny added and pushed to her feet. "I'll help."

Kiera and Nash were again left alone in the living room. She gave Heather some toys from the diaper bag to keep her busy and then turned to Nash. "I have something for you."

"What's that?"

She reached up behind her head, unclasped the chain holding the gold cross and held it out to him. "You said to bring this home to you."

He nodded, swallowed and cleared his throat. Rather

than taking the cross, however, he pressed it into her palm and closed her fingers around it. "Keep it."

"Nash."

"For now," he added. "And if we're separated again for any reason, then give me the cross, and I'll bring it home to you. It can be the thing that tethers us when we're apart and always reunites us."

She liked that. "All right."

"I'm going to do my best to make you and Heather happy."

"You already have."

She couldn't help marveling at how her life had changed in such a short period of time. She'd gone from living in fear and in constant danger to embarking on a life with the man of her dreams.

As they embraced, Kiera envisioned the path that lay ahead for her and Nash. It shined bright with promise and joy and, at long last, peace of mind.

God was indeed gracious and had shined His light on them.

* * * * *

LOVE INSPIRED

Stories to uplift and inspire

Fall in love with Love Inspired—
inspirational and uplifting stories of faith
and hope. Find strength and comfort in
the bonds of friendship and community.
Revel in the warmth of possibility and the
promise of new beginnings.

Sign up for the Love Inspired newsletter
at **LoveInspired.com** to be the first
to find out about upcoming titles,
special promotions and exclusive content.

CONNECT WITH US AT:

Facebook.com/LoveInspiredBooks

Twitter.com/LoveInspiredBks

Get 4 FREE REWARDS!

We'll send you 2 FREE Books plus 2 FREE Mystery Gifts.

FREE
Value Over
$20

Both the **Love Inspired®** and **Love Inspired®** Suspense series feature compelling novels filled with inspirational romance, faith, forgiveness, and hope.

YE$! Please send me 2 FREE novels from the Love Inspired or Love Inspired Suspense series and my 2 FREE gifts (gifts are worth about $10 retail). After receiving them, if I don't wish to receive any more books, I can return the shipping statement marked "cancel." If I don't cancel, I will receive 6 brand-new Love Inspired Larger-Print books or Love Inspired Suspense Larger-Print books every month and be billed just $6.24 each in the U.S. or $6.49 each in Canada. That is a savings of at least 17% off the cover price. It's quite a bargain! Shipping and handling is just 50¢ per book in the U.S. and $1.25 per book in Canada.* I understand that accepting the 2 free books and gifts places me under no obligation to buy anything. I can always return a shipment and cancel at any time by calling the number below. The free books and gifts are mine to keep no matter what I decide.

Choose one: ☐ **Love Inspired**
Larger-Print
(122/322 IDN GRDF)

☐ **Love Inspired Suspense**
Larger-Print
(107/307 IDN GRDF)

Name (please print)

Address   Apt. #

City   State/Province   Zip/Postal Code

Email: Please check this box ☐ if you would like to receive newsletters and promotional emails from Harlequin Enterprises ULC and its affiliates. You can unsubscribe anytime.

Mail to the Harlequin Reader Service:

IN U.S.A.: P.O. Box 1341, Buffalo, NY 14240-8531

IN CANADA: P.O. Box 603, Fort Erie, Ontario L2A 5X3

Want to try 2 free books from another series! Call 1-800-873-8635 or visit www.ReaderService.com.

HARLEQUIN
PLUS

Announcing a **BRAND-NEW**
multimedia subscription service
for romance fans like you!

Read, Watch and Play.

Experience the easiest way to get
the romance content you crave.

Start your **FREE 7 DAY TRIAL** at
<u>www.harlequinplus.com/freetrial</u>.

SPECIAL EXCERPT FROM

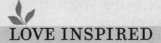

LOVE INSPIRED

*Treasured books hidden in a bookstore hold the
keys to her past.*

Read on for a sneak preview of
The Bookshop of Secrets *by Mollie Rushmeyer,
available October 2022 from Love Inspired Trade.*

Only the sharp clang of a bell above the door and lopsided towers of books greeted Hope Sparrow as she entered the bookshop Dusty Jackets.

She breathed in the ancient paper dust, the gentle decay. Between pages like these, she'd always found her refuge.

Her Lucy Maud, Jane, the sisters Brontë, dear Louisa—all whispered the words she'd pored over in the dead of night and now fortified her strength for what she hoped was the last leg in a long journey.

"Hello? Anyone here?" She strode to the empty wooden sales counter, blew out a slow, steadying breath and sat her tattered cloth suitcase containing all of her worldly possessions at her feet.

In a rounded alcove, a silky black cat snoozed atop a precarious sun-drenched stack of tomes. Nothing stirred in the transformed Victorian home, where every available space held piles of books resembling mini Leaning Towers of Pisa.

"Austenite." A voice creaked in the still air.

She whirled around. A tuft of white hair bobbed between the book pillars.

She moved closer. "Excuse me?"

"I said, Austenite." A small older man popped out from behind a pile of now-obsolete—or so she assumed—encyclopedias. "I'd know one anywhere. It's the buttoned-up self-satisfaction."

She put a hand to the tidy bun at the nape of her neck, and her lips tugged at the corners. "Guilty. Though I prefer the melancholy beauty of Charlotte Brontë's moors or Lucy Montgomery's charming Prince Edward Island."

The man beamed and stuck out his hand. She shook it, trying to hide the anxiety human touch brought on. "I couldn't agree more. I'm Ulysses Barrick. I co-own Dusty Jackets with my wife, Margaret. Welcome to Wanishin Falls. I hope Lake Superior and her steely gray wiles are treating you well. And, love, you are…?"

"I'm Hope Sparrow. I understand you're—were—the brother of Agatha O'Brien. She was a good friend of mine, and I think she sent some very special books for you to hang on to until I was able to collect them."

Don't miss
The Bookshop of Secrets *by Mollie Rushmeyer,*
available October 2022
wherever Love Inspired books and ebooks are sold.

LoveInspired.com

LITREXP0922